"I'm taking this situation very seriously," Hunter said.

"The whole team is," he continued. "We'll figure out how you were found and make sure it doesn't happen again."

Annie wanted to believe him, but nothing had happened the way it was supposed to in the past year. She blinked back tears.

A new year. No more tears over things she couldn't change. She was going to make her life what she wanted it to be. What she thought God wanted it to be.

"I won't let anything happen to your baby. I promise," Hunter said.

Please keep your promise, Hunter.

* * *

WITNESS PROTECTION: Hiding in plain sight

Books by Shirlee McCoy

SHIRLEE McCOY

has always loved making up stories. As a child, she daydreamed elaborate tales in which she was the heroine—gutsy, strong and invincible. Though she soon grew out of her superhero fantasies, her love for storytelling never diminished. She knew early that she wanted to write inspirational fiction, and she began writing her first novel when she was a teenager. Still, it wasn't until her third son was born that she truly began pursuing her dream of being published. Three years later, she sold her first book. Now a busy mother of five, Shirlee is a homeschooling mom by day and an inspirational author by night. She and her husband and children live in the Pacific Northwest and share their house with a dog, two cats and a bird. You can visit her website, www.shirleemccoy.com, or email her at shirlee@shirleemccoy.com.

SAFE BY THE MARSHAL'S SIDE

SHIRLEE McCOY

HARLEQUIN® LOVE INSPIRED® SUSPENSE

Special thanks and acknowledgment
to Shirlee McCoy for her contribution to the
Witness Protection miniseries.

Recycling programs
for this product may
not exist in your area.

 ™ LOVE INSPIRED BOOKS

ISBN-13: 978-0-373-67589-0

SAFE BY THE MARSHAL'S SIDE

Copyright © 2014 by Harlequin Books S.A.

For in the day of trouble he will keep me safe in his dwelling; he will hide me in the shelter of his sacred tent and set me high upon a rock.
—*Psalms* 27:5

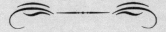

With much thanks to a fantastic group of writers—
Margaret Daley, Sharon Dunn, Liz Johnson,
Valerie Hansen and Terri Reed.
You ladies are awesome!

ONE

"Three, two, one. Happy New Year to me," Annie Duncan muttered as she flicked off the television. 12:00 a.m. on the first day of the New Year. She hoped *this* year would be better than the last one had been.

"At least it can't be any worse," she sighed as she walked down the hallway that led to the room she shared with her daughter. Sophia could have had her own bedroom, but Annie wasn't ready for that. Not yet.

She eased the door open and stepped into the room. The house was older than the one they'd had during the year they'd spent in Milwaukee, the wood floor creaky and cool under her feet. Sophia lay in her crib, her little toes peeking out from beneath the blanket, the stuffed dog that Joe had bought when Annie learned she was pregnant clutched in her arms.

Sophia was such a beautiful little girl. Joe would

have been so excited to see her as a toddler, hear her baby-babble change to words and sentences.

He'd loved their daughter. Annie could still say that, and she still believed it. Even if so many other things in their lives had been lies.

She touched Sophia's soft baby curls, as the sound of quiet conversation drifted from the room below. She didn't tense the way she had her first few weeks back in St. Louis. She'd gotten used to having people in the house with her twenty-four hours a day. The U.S. Marshals had made it as easy on her and Sophia as they could. The two-story safe house had been fitted with security systems and monitors, the upper level where she and Sophia spent most of their time perfect for their small family. It felt homey, but it wasn't home.

Annie wasn't sure when they would have that again.

Even Christmas hadn't made the place feel any less like a comfortable hotel, a stopping point on the way to somewhere else. Poor Sophia. Her third Christmas had been a bust. For the most part, the marshals who were guarding them had left them alone. They'd spent the day together. Just the two of them. That was the way it had been since their return to St. Louis. Aside from an occasional trip to meet with prosecuting attorney Steven Antonio, Annie and Sophia hung out together. That was fine and fun for a twenty-six-month-old, but Annie was starting to crave adult company and companionship.

Just a few more weeks and the case against the men who'd murdered her husband would be over. She could go back to Milwaukee or head to some new town, some new adventure. The lead marshal working her case had assured her that she'd be safe once the trial was over. She trusted Hunter Davis. He'd helped her through the tough times after Joe's murder, traveled with her from her hometown of St. Louis to Milwaukee to ease her transition into her new life.

Of course, she'd trusted Joe, too, and look where that had gotten her.

One way or another, she was going to follow through on her agreement to testify against Luke Saunders and John Fiske. She owed it to Joe, she owed it to the marshals who'd been protecting her, but mostly she owed it to Sophia. Someday, she was going to ask about her father. Annie wanted to be able to say she'd done everything possible to make sure his murderers were put in jail.

There were other things she wouldn't say until Sophia was much older, things that had surprised Annie, upset her, made her question everything she'd believed about her husband.

"He was a good guy with a problem," she whispered, but saying it out loud couldn't make it true. Sometimes she wondered if he really *had* been a good guy or if she'd just been so in love that she'd been blinded to what lay in the depths of his heart.

She walked to the window that overlooked the backyard. Snow had fallen earlier in the day, just a light dusting that she would have loved to bring Sophia out in. Hunter had refused to allow it. He was one of the most stubborn men Annie had ever met. Emotionless and by the book, he loved to tell her how things were going to be. She always did what he said because she couldn't risk Sophia's life and he seemed to know how to protect it.

She leaned her forehead against the cold glass, wishing she dared go against Hunter's order to stay inside at all times. A little fresh air would be nice. She was too much of a chicken to risk it, though.

She hadn't always been afraid.

As a matter of fact, she used to think her life was going to be wonderful. She'd married her high school sweetheart, had a baby, planned to return to her preschool teaching job when Sophia was old enough to attend. Money had been tight, but that hadn't bothered her. She'd been happy, excited to see what life would bring.

Now...

She glanced at Sophia, her stomach churning with anxiety. She just wanted to feel safe again and to believe that her daughter was safe.

"Please, Lord, don't let anything happen to her," she prayed as she turned back to the window.

There was nothing to look at. Just the wide expanse of the yard. The landscaping was basic—grass and a few low shrubs. A small swing set stood in the far corner of the yard. In the month that they'd been there, Sophia hadn't been allowed to toddle around in the grass or sit in the baby swing.

Guilt settled like a heavy weight on Annie's shoulders. All she'd ever wanted was to be a wife and mother. She'd spent her childhood dreaming of having a houseful of kids. Joe hadn't been sure he'd wanted any, but he'd finally agreed that one or two would be nice.

After Sophia's birth, he'd said that being a father was the best thing that had ever happened to him.

Her eyes filled at the memory, her chest tight with grief. Even after learning about his lies, she missed Joe.

Clouds drifted across the moon, shrouding the yard in deeper darkness. A six-foot fence surrounded the property, the houses to either side well lit. Annie imagined friends and families gathered together to greet the New Year, and she felt more alone than ever.

She hadn't spoken to her parents in over a year, hadn't seen any of her friends in that same amount of time. She'd spent a month in hiding in a little house in St. Louis not far from where she'd grown up, and she hadn't been allowed to let anyone she loved know it. She was tired and bored out of her mind, ready to break free, do something fun, be with people who cared about her.

"Stop it," she muttered. "Things could be a lot worse."

As if her words had conjured trouble, a dark shadow rose above the fence. She blinked, sure that her eyes were playing tricks on her. The shadow remained just at the corner of the fence where the safe-house yard butted up against the neighbors' yards. Head, shoulders, arms. A person. A man? A quick furtive movement and something dark rolled into the yard.

Annie's heart jumped, her body cold with fear. She'd been warned that the men she planned to testify against were dangerous. She'd been told that they'd go to any length necessary to silence her. She'd seen what they'd done to Joe, but she'd been safe for a year, going about her life in Milwaukee without even a hint of danger.

Sophia!

She had to protect her daughter. She ran to the baby, lifting her from the bed in one quick movement. Her hands shook as she fumbled with the blanket and tucked it around her daughter. She raced into the hallway, the sound of feet pounding on stairs echoing through the quiet house.

The door that led from the rooms below into her upstairs apartment burst open, and Hunter Davis appeared. Tall, with broad shoulders and a granite-hard face, he wore dark jeans, a dark T-shirt and a gun holster strapped to his chest.

"We're leaving," he said without preamble, taking her arm, his grip hard without being painful.

"Someone was at the back fence," she told him, even though she was sure he already knew. He wasn't the kind of guy to miss things.

"That's why we're moving you and Sophia out."

"But—"

"Annie," he said quietly. "I've been doing this for a long time, and I haven't lost a witness yet."

"There's always a first time for everything."

"This won't be it," he responded with confidence.

"Hunter, I—"

"Trust me, okay? That'll make it a lot easier for me to do my job." He led her down the stairway and into the lower-level apartment. Unlike the upstairs, it was sparsely furnished. Just a couch and a couple of chairs, a desk set up with a computer monitor. Two people hovered near it, watching an image on the screen. She knew both of them. U.S. marshals Burke Trier and Joshua McCall. They'd been part of her twenty-four-hour protection for the past month.

"No movement," Burke said, his dark gaze shooting to Annie. "Whatever he tossed into the yard is still there. The bomb squad will be here in five."

Hunter was glad to hear it. In the month since Angel Delacorte, now called Annie, had returned to St. Louis, they'd kept her and little Sophia locked away in the safe house. As the lead witness against Luke Saunders and John Fiske, Annie had the potential to bring down an organized crime ring that had been working out of St. Louis for the past several years. The FBI suspected that Saunders and Fiske were low-level members of the group, and the marshals had been asked to get Annie to trial safely. They'd changed her name to Annie Duncan, flown her to Milwaukee and kept her safe there.

So far, things had gone according to the plan Hunter helped create.

It looked as though that was about to change.

"We're going into the garage," he said, meeting Annie's dark blue eyes. "I'll put Sophia into her car seat. You get into the backseat beside her."

She didn't question his orders.

Good. They didn't have time to argue or to go over the plan again. He took the baby from Annie's arms. Not really a baby. A toddler with her mother's thick dark curls and big blue eyes. Pretty and delicate and filled with childish enthusiasm. After a year of working the Delacorte case and a month of spending most of his working hours protecting them, he knew little Sophia well. She didn't make a sound as he set her into the car seat, just stuck her thumb in her mouth and smiled around it.

"Good girl," he murmured, snapping the straps into place. Making sure Annie made it to trial and didn't change her mind about testifying was his job.

Simple as that. He'd done the same with dozens of other witnesses.

There was something different about this assignment, though.

Maybe the little girl who went along with it. Maybe her mother. Despite the trouble Annie was in, despite losing her husband, giving up her job, giving up all contact with her family, she'd managed to hold on to a positive attitude. That made it easy to guard her. It had probably also made it easy for her husband to pull the wool over her eyes.

Her vision was clear now, though. After months of investigation, Joe Delacorte's secret life had been revealed. Joe's murder hadn't been random. He hadn't walked in on a robbery; he'd been killed because he couldn't pay back what he'd owed. Annie hadn't said a word when the prosecutor told her how much money her husband had borrowed to feed his gambling addiction.

Hunter was pretty sure she'd cried that night.

Her eyes had been red-rimmed the next day, but she'd still had a smile on her face when she'd greeted him.

She wasn't smiling now.

She looked terrified, her face stark white.

He almost patted her arm and told her everything would be okay, but he liked to keep some distance between himself and the witnesses he protected. He didn't want to ever have his judgment and instincts skewed by useless emotion.

He tapped his finger on the steering wheel, waiting impatiently for the all clear. Serena Summers should be outside by now, checking the perimeters, making sure that it was safe to leave.

He frowned at the thought. She'd changed since her brother's murder. A fellow marshal, Daniel Summers had been killed in the line of duty. A year after his death, they still had no suspects, no useful leads, nothing that would bring his murderer to justice.

"What are we waiting for?" Annie asked quietly, her tone soft and easy, just the way it always was. Whatever stress she was feeling, whatever fear, it wasn't in her voice.

"Just waiting for an all clear," he replied, shifting in his seat to look her in the eyes. "You and Sophia won't be coming back here."

"I know."

"I'll grab some of your things later. What do you want me to get?"

"Sophia's going to want the stuffed dog her daddy gave her. The little brown one with the floppy ears. It's on her bed."

"What about you?"

She shrugged, thick strands of dark hair sliding across her shoulder. "I have a small suitcase in the closet. It's packed with clothes and baby supplies."

From what he'd observed in the past month, that

was typical of Annie. Organized, prepared. "I'll make sure to grab it for you."

"Thanks. Why do you think it's taking so long for the all clear? Do you think someone is outside waiting for us to leave?" she asked, glancing at the garage door.

"I don't know, but we're not going to take any chances." He kept the answer brief, his body tense and ready for whatever action he needed to take. Drive away or go back into the house—either option would work. As long as it kept Annie and Sophia safe.

His radio crackled, Serena's voice filling the quiet SUV.

"It's all clear," she said. "No sign of trouble out front."

"We're on our way. You're following us to the next place?" He didn't give any indication of where they were going, didn't want to take a chance that someone had somehow tapped into their conversation.

"I'll be right behind you," Serena said.

He stabbed at the garage door opener and pulled out of the garage. Darkness pressed in on the SUV windows, the trees and grass white with ice. It was the first morning of the New Year, the streetlights pouring soft yellow light onto the road and the ice-coated foliage. It would have been beautiful if Hunter hadn't been so convinced that danger was lurking just out of sight. He could feel it, his skin tight with adrenaline, his senses alive. Every shadow, every swaying branch or rustling leaf hinted at trouble.

Across the street, headlights flashed. Serena signaling from her unmarked car. They'd worked as a team before. Despite her grief and anger over Daniel's death, Hunter trusted Serena to do her job and do it well.

He glanced in the rearview mirror, met Annie's eyes.

"It's going to be okay," he said, because he thought she needed the reassurance.

She nodded.

She probably didn't believe him. He couldn't blame her. She'd been promised that she'd be safe in St. Louis, told that she wouldn't be found, that she and her daughter had nothing to fear. He'd said all those things to her on the plane ride back from Milwaukee. They should have been true.

Someone had found Annie, though.

Who?

How?

That was the better question.

No one but marshals working the case knew where the safe house was located. Hunter had gone to incredible lengths to make sure they weren't followed when he brought Annie to her appointments with prosecuting attorneys. Long rides out into the country and back, circuitous routes through the heart of downtown—all of it designed to throw off a tail or to spot one.

There'd been no indication that they'd been followed, but the safe house had been compromised. Logical reason dictated that someone had leaked the information, but Hunter wanted to think anything other than that.

Too bad he couldn't.

He rubbed the back of his neck, glad that Annie was keeping her thoughts to herself. It was probably tempting to throw accusations. After all, she was doing the feds a favor by testifying. She'd been promised a lot of things that had made Hunter cringe. Things that could never really be promised—a new life, a new home, a chance to put the past behind her and to put her husband's killers in jail.

All Hunter had promised was that he'd keep her safe.

He intended to do that.

Nothing and no one was going to keep that from happening.

TWO

One hour and five minutes.

That was how long Annie had been sitting silently in the back of Hunter's SUV. Sophia had drifted off to sleep minutes after the ride began. Annie wished she could fall asleep as easily. She was exhausted, but too wound up and scared to close her eyes.

Hunter had said everything would be okay, but it didn't feel okay. It felt as if she was running away again, killers on her trail.

An image flashed through her head—blood on old linoleum. Joe gasping for breath. She thought she could smell the sharp scent of gunfire in the air.

"Where are we going?" she asked. Anything to stop the memories.

"Another safe house," Hunter responded tersely. He'd been on his radio twice since they'd left the safe house. Neither conversation had made him happy. Not enough information to go on. That was what he'd told her when she'd asked for an update on what had been thrown into the safe-house yard.

That hadn't surprised her. In the time that she'd known him, he'd proved to be a man of few words. Usually that didn't bother her. Live and let live. That was the way her parents had raised her. Be kind, be patient, show love. Those had been the tenets of their faith, and they were the keystones of Annie's, too.

Right at that moment, though, she was out of patience with Hunter. "Can you be a little more specific?"

"No."

"Why not?"

"It's better if you don't know the address."

That seemed to be his argument for everything. *It's better if you stay inside. It's better if you don't call your family. It's better if you sit in the back of my car and be quiet and let me figure everything out.*

"It's not like I'm going to tell anyone where we're going."

"I know."

"Then tell me. I'm an adult. I have a child. I think I have the right to know."

"You picked a bad night to assert yourself, Annie."

"The way I see it, I should have asserted myself a long time ago," she replied. She'd spent a year going by a new name, living as a different person and doing absolutely everything Hunter had told her to do. She hadn't questioned him because she'd wanted to protect Sophia.

The baby. Don't let anything happen to the baby.

Joe had gasped those words with his last breath. Late at night, when it was quiet and dark, they'd echo in Annie's head until she had to get up and touch Sophia's cheek, make sure that she was okay.

"Only you can decide that," he said calmly. "But for the record, I'm following protocol. That's what's kept you safe for a year."

"You're not the only one who wants to keep me safe, Hunter. I have a vested interest in it, too. I have a baby who needs me. I have to make sure I'm around for her."

"She's not really a baby anymore, is she?" he asked. "A couple of days ago, she said my name. Clear as day."

He was trying to distract her. A new move for Hunter. He usually stuck to facts and figures and orders. Maybe he sensed how close to the edge of panic she was.

Her parents had told her not to testify.

They'd begged her to move to a new town, stay away from St. Louis and forget what she'd seen. They'd been afraid that if she agreed to testify, she'd end up like Joe. At the time, Annie had thought that Joe had been an innocent bystander, a guy who'd gotten in the way of a robbery and been killed because of it. She'd wanted nothing more than to see his killers thrown in jail, so she'd refused her parents' advice.

She'd received a lot of new information since then, but she still wanted the men who'd killed her husband to pay for their crimes.

"Someone found me at the safe house, Hunter," she finally said. "Talking about Sophia won't change that."

"I know, but I thought it might help you relax." He glanced into the rearview mirror, offering a rare smile. It changed his face, made him less austere and more approachable.

"It's hard to relax when someone wants me dead."

"We don't know that there's a price on your head."

"But you think that Saunders and Fiske want to keep me from testifying against them. You told me that if they killed Joe, they wouldn't hesitate to kill me." She'd believed him because she'd seen the look in Luke Saunders's eyes after he'd shot Joe. Triumph. Excitement. Just thinking about it made her stomach churn.

"Unless they've been able to arrange for the hit from their prison cells, what happened tonight could just be—"

"I saw the person at the back fence. I know something was tossed into the yard. Don't try to tell me that it was some New Year's reveler. I'm not going to believe it."

"I wouldn't lie to you, Annie," he said quietly, and she thought that he probably meant it.

But Joe had said the same thing so many times, she'd almost stopped hearing it. He'd said it when checks bounced or electricity bills weren't paid. He'd said it when she'd asked why he was home late from work or why their money always seemed to disappear.

She'd believed every lie he'd told her.

She wouldn't make that mistake again. Not with anyone. Even a guy who seemed to be honorable.

"Everyone lies sometimes," she responded. "And you getting me to relax isn't a solution to our problem."

"Trust me, I know that. I'm taking this situation very seriously. The whole team is. We'll figure out how you were found, and we'll make sure it doesn't happen again."

She wanted to believe him, but nothing had happened the way it was supposed to in the past year. She blinked back tears. She'd cried an ocean of them since Joe's death. Every time she thought she was cried out, more tears came.

Not this time, though.

A new year. A new beginning. No more tears over things she couldn't change. She was going to take control, make her life what she wanted it to be. What she thought *God* wanted it to be.

Hunter turned down a well-lit street lined with

tall apartment buildings. Not as quiet as the street the safe house had been on. Lights shone from most of the apartment windows and a few people milled around in a small courtyard between two buildings.

Hunter bypassed the taller apartment complexes and pulled into the parking garage of a four-story building that sat on a small corner lot. Several cars filled spaces in the dark enclave. He parked near a door, shifting in his seat and looking straight into Annie's eyes.

He had the darkest eyes she'd ever seen, his eyelashes thick and just as dark. She didn't know why she was noticing. Maybe because it was easier than thinking about getting out of the SUV with Sophia, walking through the parking garage and into the building, the hot breath of danger still on her neck.

"What are we doing?" she whispered as if someone outside the SUV might hear.

"Waiting for Marshal Summers."

Annie knew the woman. She'd been at the safe house several times in the past month, her dark hair pulled back, her brown eyes kind. They hadn't spoken much. Just a few hellos and goodbyes. Not enough to get to know her well.

A black sedan pulled into the space beside them, and Serena Summers got out. All business in dark slacks and a heavy coat, she opened Annie's door and gestured for her to get out. "Let's go. I don't know about you, but *I'll* feel a lot better once you're inside that building."

"I need to get Sophia." She reached for the car-seat buckle, but Hunter was already opening the door on Sophia's side.

"I'll get her. You go with Serena."

"But—"

"I won't let anything happen to her. I promise," he said.

Don't promise me anything, she wanted to say.

But he was already unbuckling Sophia.

Arguing out in the open where anyone could see her seemed even more foolish than trusting him to take care of Sophia. Besides, she might have learned hard lessons about trust from her marriage, but she knew Hunter would do everything he could to protect Sophia. She just hoped it was enough.

She got out of the SUV and hurried into the building with Serena. The place was quiet, any tenants tucked behind closed doors. Two elevators stood on the far wall of a brightly lit foyer. Serena led her there, sliding a card into a slot next to one of the doors, her foot tapping as she waited for it to open.

As soon as it did, she urged Annie in, holding the door open as Hunter hurried in behind them. Sophia snuggled in his arms, her head against his shoulder, her thumb in her mouth. She smiled sleepily as she saw Annie.

"Momma, hold me!" she said, her little arms reaching for Annie.

Annie took her from Hunter's arms, loving the solid weight of her. She didn't think she'd really known the depth of God's love for her until Sophia came along.

"Where's we going?" Sophia asked, pressing her hand to Annie's cheek and looking into her eyes.

Joe would have been so excited to hear her talk. He'd been longing for the day when she would say more than *Dada, Momma* and the few other words she'd perfected in the months before he was killed. Now she could, and he was gone, undone by his gambling addiction, murdered by men he'd owed money to.

Her throat tightened at the thought, the tears she'd decided not to shed burning the backs of her eyes.

"A new house," she responded, her voice thick and watery.

The elevator doors opened, and Hunter took her elbow, leading her into a wide corridor. His fingers seemed to burn through her long-sleeved T-shirt, the feeling so surprising, she shrugged away.

Hunter let Annie go. There was no need to be overly protective. The five apartments on this floor were empty, each one secretly rented by the U.S. Marshals. It was easier that way. No danger of tenants seeing a high-profile witness and leaking the news to the press. No need to do background checks on people who rented the apartments.

Serena used her key to open the door at the end of the hall. The place hadn't been used in over a year. There'd be a layer of dust on everything and an air of neglect that couldn't be helped. He knew Annie wouldn't complain. She never did. He still wished they'd had time to make the apartment a little more kid-friendly. Some toys. Safety covers on outlets. A crib.

He frowned.

They'd need to improvise for the night. Tomorrow, he'd buy one of those portable cribs his sister used for her son.

"Here we are," Serena announced as she flicked on a light. "Home sweet home until the trial."

It didn't really look like a home. Just a couch and a coffee table. No throw rug on the wood floor. No pictures on the wall. A small galley kitchen connected to the living area, the appliances stainless steel, the cupboards white. It was fancier than the little house Annie had lived in before entering witness protection. Hunter knew that for a fact. He'd seen pictures of the crime scene. The kitchen with its mustard-colored appliances and peeling linoleum floor. Thanks to her husband, Annie hadn't had much to brag about.

Hunter didn't think she was the kind of person who cared. Still, if he ever got married, he'd want to do a lot better for his family than a run-down house in a questionable neighborhood. He knew that wasn't possible for some people, but Joe Delacorte had made enough money to provide for his family. He'd just preferred to spend it gambling.

"The place could use a little cleaning," Serena said, running her finger through a layer of dust on the granite counter that separated the living room from the kitchen. "Sorry, Annie. I didn't have enough notice to get it done."

"It's okay." Annie set Sophia down, smiling a little as her daughter toddled across the room. "But, unless this place is outfitted for a toddler, I'm going to need a couple of things before morning."

"Like?" Serena pulled out a small notebook. Obviously, she was ready to make a list and head out to find whatever was needed. He could have told her exactly what Annie would ask for. Diapers, baby wipes, apple juice and some sort of toasted oat cereal for Sophia to snack on. Nothing for herself.

Hunter walked down a narrow hall and opened the first door to the left. A master bedroom with an attached bathroom, it had a wide window that looked out over an alley. A queen-size bed sat against one wall. A dresser stood in front of another. He flicked on the light in the bathroom, ran the water in the sink and tub just to make sure everything was in working order.

There were towels in a small linen closet. Soap. Shampoo. None of it for babies.

"Hey, Hunter!" Serena called. "I'm going to see if I can round up some supplies. I'll be back as soon as possible."

"It might be difficult to find a place open, but don't go back to the other location. We don't want to clutter the scene," he responded as he walked back into the living room.

Annie had settled onto the floor, Sophia spinning in circles beside her. The little girl's giggles made him smile. He'd always loved kids, but his life was too busy, his job too demanding to think about having a family of his own.

"The local Walmart will probably be open. If it's not, I'll stop at a convenience store. I can at least get—" Serena consulted her list, stabbing at one of the items. "Diapers, wet wipes and Cheerios. The rest I can pick up tomorrow."

"I'll radio you any information that comes in." He glanced at his watch. So far, there'd been little to go on. The bomb squad had arrived at the safe house within minutes and converged on a gift-wrapped package that had been found in the yard. No explosives, but the team wasn't taking any chances. They'd bagged the package and transported it to their forensic lab. It would be opened there, everything handled in a sterile environment so there'd be no risk of contaminating evidence.

Serena walked out of the apartment, and Hunter slid the bolt home. The apartment's second bedroom was set up with a computer that was hooked into the building's security system. He could monitor the exterior of the building from there. They hadn't been followed. He was sure of that, but it didn't give him any peace.

Annie had been found once. There was no reason to think she wouldn't be found again.

"I've got some work to do. If you need anything, let me know," he said. He sounded cold and uncaring. He knew it. It wasn't the way he meant to come off, but years of following the rules, of shoving his emotions down so that he could do his job effectively had taken their toll.

Another good reason to not pursue the kind of relationship that led to love and marriage. A few dates a year with nice women who were as career-driven as he was had been enough for so many years he'd lost track.

Somehow, though, every year when Christmas and the New Year rolled around, he started thinking about having more, about what his life would be like if he'd made different decisions and chosen a different path.

Too much time with his sister Carrie and her family, that was the problem. She and her husband, Mitch, were happy, their four children thriving. During the holidays, their house was filled with the kind of joy that washed over everyone who entered.

Yeah. It made him want more than the house he shared with coworker Burke Trier, but that didn't mean he could have it. God would have to drop a very special woman into his life for things to change. He knew that from watching his parents. His father had been a trauma surgeon, his life devoted to his career. His mother had been sad, then frustrated, then, ultimately, resentful. No way did Hunter want to hurt a woman the way his father had unwittingly hurt his mother.

He shrugged off the thought and walked down the hall. He could hear Sophia's giggles and Annie's low murmur as he logged in to the security system. They were more distracting than he wanted them to be. As a matter of fact, if he'd let himself, he could have happily gone back into the living room and spent a little time with the young widow and her child. The two had been through a lot, and they deserved to feel secure and cared for.

His cell phone rang, and he answered.

"Davis speaking."

"It's Josh. I'm at the evidence lab. The technicians are finished with the box."

"What was in it?" He tensed, anxious to hear what had been discovered.

"A doll."

"A *doll?*" He glanced at the doorway and saw that Annie was hovering there, Sophia in her arms.

"One without a head. There was a note included. It was addressed to Sophia Delacorte. It said, 'Don't tell.'"

"So, our safe house *was* compromised," he muttered. He'd known it the moment he'd seen the shadow rise above the fence, but this proved it absolutely.

"Looks that way. We brought in a dog to track the perpetrator but the K-9 team lost the trail a half mile from the safe house."

"He had a ride." Had probably spent hours planning things. If he couldn't get to Annie, he could try to scare her enough to get her to change her mind about testifying.

Hunter gestured for Annie to enter the room as he said goodbye to Josh.

"It's bad news, isn't it?" she asked.

"Just someone trying to scare you, Annie. But you don't need to be afraid."

"Because you're going to keep us safe?" She kissed her daughter's forehead, but her eyes were sharp, her expression harder than he'd ever seen it.

"Yes."

"How?"

"The same way I have been. Keeping you in the safe house until the trial."

"It didn't work that well the last time. What makes you think this time will be any different?"

"It did work. You and Sophia were never in danger," he tried to reassure her.

"Then why did it feel like we were?" She sounded exasperated and scared.

"This is all routine, Annie. My team is handling it."

She shrugged, and he could see the doubt in her eyes. She let it drop, though. "You said something about a doll. What were you talking about?"

He explained briefly, watching as she paled. She had a few freckles on her cheeks and nose, and her eyes were deep sapphire-blue. The first time he'd seen her, he'd thought she was about sixteen, she'd looked so young.

She was older than that by a decade, but she still gave off a young and innocent vibe, a naïveté that made him worry more than he probably should about what she would do and where she would go after she finished testifying.

"Sophia's doll was missing," she said, her voice tight.

Her comment chased every other thought away. "What doll? When did it go missing?"

"Right after Joe died. I looked everywhere for it when I was packing things to take to Milwaukee. I thought maybe Joe had put it somewhere the night he was…" She shook her head.

"What did the doll look like?"

"It was a rag doll. Nothing expensive. Just all cloth with dark hair and dark eyes. Joe bought it for Sophia's first birthday. I made a pink dress for it."

"Sophia was at a sitter's house the night your husband was killed, wasn't she?" he asked. He knew the facts, but sometimes revisiting them helped witnesses recall details that they hadn't before. This was the first he'd heard about a doll, and he wanted to hear more.

"Yes."

"Could the doll have been left there?"

"The sitter said Sophia didn't have it with her. I think Joe rushed while he was packing her bag and forgot it. Usually, I was the one..." She pressed her lips together. "Sorry. I'm rambling."

"How about you let me decide if that's the case? You usually did what?"

"Packed Sophia's diaper bag. Joe wasn't very good at remembering what she needed, but since she wasn't supposed to be at the sitter's that night, I didn't bother."

"That's right. You thought she was going to be at home, didn't you?"

"Yes." She frowned. "I'm glad she wasn't, though. Things could have turned out even worse."

True. But was she glad she'd been lied to?

Was she glad her husband, who was supposed to

be caring for their child, had probably been planning to do a little gambling while his wife was away?

A little?

The guy had been knee-deep in debt with no way of getting out of it.

Hunter didn't mention that.

It would have been like rubbing salt in an open wound.

Besides, Annie was right—if Sophia *had* been home, she might have been hurt. Or worse. "You're sure the doll didn't go with her to the sitter? Maybe with all the trauma—"

"Sophia was crying for it." She cut him off, her eyes flashing with irritation. "The sitter left a message for Joe asking him to bring it. I didn't know about the message until months later since the police confiscated our answering machine. There's a transcript if you're interested."

"You're angry," he pointed out, and she frowned.

"No, I'm upset. I'm frustrated. I want my life back. I am *not* angry."

"Okay," he agreed.

He'd have been angry. He'd have wanted a little justice, too.

"Sophia is tired." She touched her daughter's dark curls. "I'm going to tuck her in for the night."

She pivoted and walked away, her hair swaying, her body hidden by a layer of faded denim and an oversize Rams sweatshirt. Was it her husband's?

Not something that concerned Hunter, but he didn't want to think that Annie was still mourning the man who'd lied to her, stolen from their family and caused her heartache on top of heartache.

"Not your business," he muttered as he turned back to the security monitor, grabbed his cell phone and dialed Joshua's number.

THREE

Annie woke with a start, her heart racing, a scream dying in her throat.

Darkness shadowed the furniture and lay deep and thick in the corners of the room. She sat up, her feet touching cool hardwood.

It took a moment to know where she was.

The safe house.

Safe *apartment*.

Not the kitchen of the little St. Louis rental she and Joe had chosen after their wedding. Not standing with a gun pointed at her head while Joe moaned on the floor, blood seeping from his chest. Night after night, she dreamed of that moment. The split second when the gun had misfired and the man who'd been pointing it at her had run.

Annie shuddered.

The sun would rise in a couple of hours. She'd feel better then, the nightmare fading, her fear fading with it.

She eased off the bed, trying not to disturb Sophia. She could hear her deep, even breathing, knew she was soundly asleep. Not hungry or scared or cold. She was a blessed little girl. Even under the circumstances. Even without a father's love. Even with the moves and the disruptions, she had more than so many children did.

Annie had tried to keep that in mind during the past year.

She paced to the window, the old wood floor creaking under her feet. Icy rain splattered against the brick facade of the building, cold air drifting in through the single pane glass. She shivered, rubbing her arms, her stomach growling. She hadn't eaten much the night before.

She thought about going to the kitchen to search for something to eat, but she didn't want to face Hunter. He'd brought her the baby supplies Serena had managed to buy, asked if she needed anything. She'd told him no, but she *had* needed something. She'd needed someone to talk to, someone who could take her mind off the nightmare she seemed to be living in.

She hadn't told him that, of course. She'd just said good-night and closed the door. Otherwise, she might have burst into tears and made a total fool of herself.

Someone knocked on the door, the soft tap barely sounding above the splattering rain.

She opened the door and found herself looking at Hunter's chest. His very muscular chest.

She blushed, looking up and meeting his dark eyes.

"Did you get the photo of the doll?" She couldn't think of any other reason for him to knock on her door at three in the morning.

"About an hour ago. I didn't think it was worth disturbing your sleep, but when I heard the floor creak, I figured you might have woken up."

"You were right." She sidled past him and walked out into the hall, her pulse racing, her cheeks still blazing. She'd known Hunter for over a year. For the past month, she'd seen him almost every day. Somehow, she'd never noticed just how masculine he was. Or maybe she had, but she hadn't wanted to admit it to herself.

"You hungry?" Hunter asked, following her as she walked into the living room. "Serena scrounged up some groceries. I'm not sure what there is. We can look around, find something to eat."

"I'd rather just see the photo." Although she had to admit, food sounded good.

"There's no reason why we can't do both."

"Except that the sun isn't even up yet."

"Should that matter?" he asked, walking into the galley kitchen and opening the refrigerator. He pulled out a package of American cheese and a carton of eggs.

Her stomach growled, and he smiled. The second smile in twenty-four hours. She was sure that was a record.

"I guess when my stomach is growling as loudly as it is, it shouldn't," she murmured.

"I'm glad you agree, because *I'm* starving."

She laughed a little at that, some of her tension easing away. "You should have eaten."

"I didn't want to make a bunch of noise in the kitchen while you were sleeping."

"You wouldn't have bothered me."

"I wasn't worried about bothering you. I was worried about waking you. Sophia is a deep sleeper. You don't seem to sleep much at all. At least you don't on any of the nights when I pull shift." He cracked several eggs in a bowl and beat them.

It was true. She hadn't been sleeping much since returning to St. Louis, but she hadn't realized that Hunter had noticed. As a matter of fact, she'd had the distinct impression that he didn't pay much attention to anything she and Sophia did. Unless he thought they were going to break a rule. Like the week before Christmas, when he'd cautioned her a half a dozen times, telling her to make sure she didn't give in to temptation and go shopping for gifts.

She hadn't actually been tempted. Celebrating Christmas without Joe had seemed too sad, too lonely. She'd been happy to give Hunter some money and a short list of gifts for Sophia.

As far as Christmases went, the last one was the worst she'd ever had.

Next year's would be better, though.

She'd promised herself that.

"You're deep in thought," Hunter said as he poured the eggs into a hot pan and dropped cheese on top of them.

"I'm just tired. Like you said, I haven't been sleeping much since I came back to St. Louis."

"Nervous about the trial?"

"Among other things."

"It's good that you have a healthy sense of caution but try not to worry too much. It's not good for you." He folded the eggs into a fluffy omelet and took a plate from the cupboard. "Are you having nightmares, too? Is that what woke you tonight?"

"Yes," she admitted. Nine nights out of ten, she woke in a cold sweat, her heart pounding with fear. She hoped that would change once Joe's murderers were in jail. Knowing both men were off the street for good would go a long way in giving her peace of mind.

"That's not surprising. You've been through some tough times. It's going to take a while to get over it," he said as he slid the omelet onto a plate and placed it in front of her. "Not that that makes the nightmares easier to deal with. Go ahead and eat while I make mine. Then I'll show you the photo of the doll."

"Okay." She stabbed at the omelet, surprised by Hunter's words. That was the most he'd ever said to her. At least, the most that he'd said that didn't have something to do with the case and her safety.

She hadn't thought he had it in him to care much about anything. Maybe she'd been wrong.

She took a bite of egg. No salt or pepper. No onions or green peppers, but it tasted good, and she really *was* hungry.

Hunter sat down across from her, a pile of scrambled eggs on his plate. He'd taken a lot more time with her food than with his own.

"Good?" he asked.

"Very. Thank you."

"No need to thank me. I'm just doing my job."

"Your job is to protect me. Not feed me."

He eyed her for a moment, his brow furrowed. "My job is to keep you healthy and safe until the trial. 'Healthy' means that you eat regular meals so that you don't fade away to nothing."

"I don't think you can call this a regular meal. It's not breakfast, lunch or dinner," she pointed out.

"It's food, and you need it. You didn't eat breakfast or dinner yesterday."

"Did you have cameras set up in the safe house?" She sounded as horrified as she felt.

"No," he said. "I checked in a couple of times

yesterday, remember? One bowl in the sink after breakfast. Two plates at lunch. Sophia's little pink plate in the sink after dinner."

"I snacked. Not that it's any of your business."

"Sure it is. Like I said, I have to—"

"Keep me healthy and safe until the trial. I know," she sighed. "Let's change the subject, okay?"

He raised one dark brow. "Why?"

"Because I'd rather talk about the doll." And because thinking about Hunter noticing all the things about her that he'd noticed made her uncomfortable. Even if he *had* just noticed because it was his job.

His dark eyes speared into hers, and, for a moment, she thought that he was going to press for more.

Finally, he stood. "I printed out a photograph. I'll get it."

She didn't follow him from the room. She needed a couple of minutes to gather her thoughts. She wanted to see the photo, but she didn't. If it *was* Sophia's doll, the men who'd murdered Joe had picked it up. She didn't remember seeing it in either of their hands, but then, she'd only caught a glimpse of John Fiske. He'd already been heading out the back door as she'd walked into the kitchen. He'd glanced over his shoulder to say something to his partner and had seen her.

Annie had been within seconds of dying that day. If the gun Luke Saunders had been carrying hadn't malfunctioned, she'd be dead. If Sophia had been home, she'd have been dead, too.

She shuddered, washing Hunter's empty plate and her own. Anything to keep the memories at bay. They were a heavy burden. One she didn't think she'd ever be able to lay down. She'd wanted so badly to save Joe. She'd pressed dishcloths to the wound in his chest, trying to sop up the blood. She'd held his hand and touched his cheek and told him he was going to be all right. She hadn't believed it. He hadn't, either.

Don't let anything happen to the baby.

His last words to her, and she'd promised that she wouldn't.

"Please, Lord, help me keep that promise. For him and for me," she whispered as she dried the plates and put them away.

The apartment floor creaked, and she knew Hunter was returning. She settled back into a chair, the eggs sitting like lead in the pit of her stomach.

Hunter took the seat across from her, sliding a folder across the table. "Are you sure you want to do this tonight?"

"It's morning, and I'm sure."

She might be sure, but her hands were trembling. Hunter noticed that and her pallor. She was ashen, her eyes bright blue in her pale face.

Any other time, any other witness, and Hunter would have been impatient for her to do what needed to be done. He *was* impatient. He needed her to look at the picture. If the doll had been taken from the Delacorte house, it would be a lot easier to connect the guy who'd used it to intimidate Annie to Saunders and Fiske. One more nail in the guys' coffins.

Once they found the person responsible.

Yeah. He was impatient, but this was Annie, and she had a softer heart than other witnesses he'd protected. So many of the people Hunter had ushered into witness protection had been criminals hiding from criminals. He hadn't felt sorry for their troubles because they'd brought them on themselves. Annie was different. Her husband had brought trouble into her life. Her only crime had been in loving a guy who'd borrowed money from the wrong people to feed his gambling addiction.

"It can wait," he said.

She shook her head. "No, it can't."

She flipped open the folder and lifted the photo.

As crime-scene photos went, it was pretty innocuous. Hunter had seen a whole lot worse than the headless doll wearing the pink dress.

Annie dropped the photo as if it was a venomous snake.

"Is it—?" Hunter started to ask.

"I need some water." She cut him off, pushing away from the table. She grabbed a glass from the cupboard, filled it at the sink, her hands shaking so hard water sloshed onto the floor.

She set the glass on the counter and grabbed the dish towel. There were tears in her eyes. He should have ignored them, kept his distance, let her clean up the water and get her emotions in check.

But she looked vulnerable and young, her shoulders slumped as she halfheartedly swiped at the drops of water. She'd given up her family to testify. Given up the friends and support system she'd had before her husband's murder.

She'd been cautioned against making too many friends in Milwaukee. Until the trial, they wanted her disconnected, free from the temptation to say too much, the danger of slipping and revealing her identity.

She had no one.

Except for him.

For some reason, that mattered to Hunter more than he wanted it to. He told himself it was because he had a younger sister, and that he'd have wanted someone to take care of her emotionally if she'd been in the same situation. He thought the reason might be a lot more complicated than that. Annie was a beautiful woman with a beautiful spirit. That was a difficult combination to resist.

He knelt beside her, took the cloth from her hand. "I'll clean it up."

"You're a U.S. marshal. Not a maid," she replied, but she scooted away and sat on the floor, her back resting against the cupboards, her arms around her knees.

"I'm whatever I need to be." He finished wiping up the water and dropped the cloth into the sink.

When she didn't move, he sat beside her. "Right now, I think you need more than a U.S. marshal. I think you need a friend."

"Don't be nice to me, okay?" Her voice broke, and she dropped her head to her knees.

"Aren't I always nice?" he responded, knowing he wasn't. Hoping the comment would make her smile.

Or at least keep her from crying.

"Nice?" She turned her head, eyeing him dispassionately. "I suppose some people would call you that."

"What would *you* call me?" he asked, more curious than he should be. She was a witness, and her opinion of him shouldn't matter. Right at that moment, though, it did.

"Efficient."

"Not hard-nosed or cold, huh?" He'd been called both on a number of occasions. He'd thought the descriptions apt and had taken them as compliments. They wouldn't be compliments coming from someone like Annie.

"No."

"That's your problem, then, Annie. You're too nice. Instead of getting mad at people who treat you badly—"

"You've never treated me badly," she cut in, and for some reason her continued kindness annoyed him. He'd rather she be like everyone else he'd protected. Convinced that he was as cold as he pretended to be.

"I've never treated you kindly, either," he pointed out. "I've done my job. That's what I get paid for, but you continue to act like I'm doing you a huge favor."

"Is that what I'm doing?" She stood, and she didn't look vulnerable or young anymore. She looked angry. "Acting?"

"That wasn't what I was saying."

"Then what were you saying, Hunter? That I'm too foolish to know that you're just here doing what you've been paid for? That I'm too stupid to realize that the only reason you're talking to me right now is because you want answers about the doll and you're afraid I'm going to have some kind of mental breakdown before I give them to you?" Her voice was soft, her tone light, but there was heat in her gaze.

"That's not why—"

"You want to know the truth? A year ago, I might have been a fool and I might have been stupid. I trusted people because I wanted to think the best of everyone. After what I learned about Joe, I'm not that naive. But that doesn't mean I can't be kind." She grabbed the folder and thrust it at him. "Yes, it's Sophia's doll. That's the dress I made for it. Check the stitching. I didn't have any pink thread so I used robin's-egg blue."

She spun on her heels and ran from the room.

She didn't slam the bedroom door, but he heard the quiet snap of the lock.

He could have followed her. It would have been easy enough to unlock the door.

But he had the answer he needed. There was no need for further conversation.

He looked down at the photo of the headless doll. The dress was intricate and well made with puffy sleeves and some sort of gathers on the front. He'd call Joshua, ask him if the thread used on the dress was blue. Just to be sure.

If it was, then the doll had been taken the night of Joe Delacorte's murder. Once they found the guy who'd tossed it into the safe-house yard, they should be able to connect him to Saunders and Fiske. Neither man would have a chance of escaping justice.

That should have excited Hunter. It was what he lived for. Seeing justice done, knowing he had done his part to make it happen.

It had always been enough before.

Right then, though, it felt empty. The thrill of the hunt, the excitement of the chase, victory in sight— none of it seemed nearly as important as making sure that Annie was okay. He hesitated, tempted to unlock Annie's door and make sure she was. He wouldn't, though. That would be crossing a line and walking into dangerous territory.

Cold detachment. It had served him well before. It would serve him well again.

He pulled out his cell phone and called Josh again.

FOUR

Annie knew she shouldn't have gotten so upset, but Hunter's attitude infuriated her. She was a grown woman with a child. Not some naive little girl. She *knew* he was doing his job. She didn't have to be reminded of the fact over and over again.

She was doing *her* job, too. Staying inside, meeting with the prosecuting attorney, sticking by her agreement to testify against Saunders and Fiske even though she couldn't help wondering if it was the right thing to do. After all, what did she really owe Joe?

In the years they'd been married, he'd apparently lied to her and stolen. He'd taken money that should have gone to their family and spent it on gambling.

She did owe Sophia, though.

A good life free of the shadows of her father's mistakes.

She touched Sophia's soft curls. Hunter had been right about one thing: Annie did need a friend. If she could have, she'd have picked up the phone and called her college roommate. Tabitha had always known the right thing to say and the right way to say it. She'd even tried to tell Annie that Joe wasn't good enough for her.

Love *was* blind. Annie hadn't seen anything but the good in Joe. She didn't want to call that a mistake. They'd had plenty of good times together, and they'd gotten Sophia from their relationship. Annie would do it all again to have her daughter.

She just wished she'd known. She wished she hadn't been so blind. Maybe then Joe would still be alive.

She tucked a strand of hair behind her ear and paced across the room. She felt antsy and trapped. No jogs in the park like she'd been able to do in Milwaukee. No trips to playgrounds. No playdates. Nothing to take her mind off the looming trial or the danger that she was in.

It was no wonder she felt irritable and unhappy.

"Annie," Hunter called, his voice soft.

Go away, she wanted to say, but she'd been raised with better manners than that. Besides, she wanted to prove that she wasn't the immature little girl he seemed to think she was.

She opened the door and stepped into the hall. "What?"

"I called Joshua. He confirmed that the thread on the doll's dress was blue."

"Okay," she said, because she'd known it would

be. She had spent hours making that little dress. She'd wanted Sophia's first doll to be something prettier than the dollar-store find Joe had brought home.

She felt guilty for thinking that.

He'd tried, and he really *had* loved Sophia. No matter how much Annie doubted everything else about her husband, she didn't doubt that.

"The crime lab is going to process the doll," Hunter continued. "Maybe we'll get some evidence that will help us find the guy who tossed it into the yard. Once we find him, we should be able to connect him to Fiske and Saunders. There's no other way he could have gotten the doll aside from one of them."

"You think that will help at trial?"

"It will be one more mark against them, and when it comes to trial, more is better."

"I hope you're right, Hunter. If they aren't convicted—"

"They will be," he assured her.

"One thing I've learned the past year, Hunter, is that there aren't any guarantees. So, I'm not going to celebrate until both men are locked away."

He nodded and leaned his shoulder against the wall. It looked as though he had more to say, but he just watched her silently.

"If that's all you wanted to say, I'm going back to bed." She put her hand on the door, not really ready to go pace the room again, but not willing to stand in the hall having a stare-down with Hunter, either.

"I owe you an apology," he said before she could close the door. "There's nothing wrong with being kind. As a matter of fact, I could use a little more practice at it."

"You've been perfectly kind," she conceded, oddly touched by his apology. For the first time since she'd met him, he seemed absolutely sincere and absolutely himself.

"For the sake of my work, sure. But I need to spend a little more time being kind for the sake of kindness." He flashed a quick smile, reached around her to push the door open. "If you're going to try to get some more sleep, you'd better do it now. Sophia is usually up at the crack of dawn."

He walked down the hall and disappeared into the kitchen.

She almost followed him. Hunter was a paradox. By the book and cold as ice, but there was something warm in him. She hadn't noticed it before, but now that she had, she couldn't seem to stop thinking about it.

Maybe that was what happened to young widows. They inevitably started noticing the men in their lives. Eventually, noticing led to falling for someone and they married again. That was what Annie's mother had said a few days after Joe's funeral.

"One day, the pain will fade. You'll find some-

one else. You'll fall in love again. You'll get married and have a dozen children," Sandy had murmured as she'd hugged Annie.

Annie hadn't believed her then, and she didn't want to believe her now. She'd learned too much about the lie her first marriage had been.

"Sorry, Mom. No marriage. No dozen children," she muttered. "Ever."

The door next to hers opened, and Serena Summers peered out, her hair pulled back into a ponytail, a few strands escaping and falling across her cheeks. "Everything okay out here?"

"Yes. Fine. I was just going back to bed."

"At…" Serena glanced at her watch. "Four in the morning? Shouldn't you already *be* in bed?"

"I was. I couldn't sleep. I probably still won't be able to, but I'm going to give it a try."

"I've been trying for three hours and haven't had any luck. Maybe we should both give in to the inevitable, drink some coffee and play a game of checkers."

"Checkers?"

Annie wasn't really in the mood for a rousing game of checkers. She wasn't really in the mood for coffee, but she couldn't *not* notice the sadness in Serena's eyes.

She saw it in her own eyes every time she looked in the mirror.

"Sounds like fun," she said and couldn't quite hide the note of sarcasm in her voice.

Serena smiled and shook her head. "Honestly, it's not my idea of fun, either. I'd rather be out on the gun range, but we're stuck here for the time being so we may as well make the best of it. Come on. I'll make the coffee."

Annie followed Serena into the small living room. Hunter was in the kitchen, so she didn't follow Serena there. Instead, she sat on the couch and waited. She wanted to ignore Hunter's presence, pretend that she hadn't noticed just how masculine he was, just how handsome. Now that she'd noticed, though, she couldn't *not* notice. She glanced his way, saw that he was watching her.

She should probably say something, but her mouth was dry, her throat tight.

"You want cream in your coffee?" Serena called, her question breaking the spell that held Annie's tongue.

"Sure. Thanks."

"Great, because that's the way I made it." Serena walked into the living room, two coffee cups balanced on a boxed checkers set. She set it on the coffee table. "Ready?"

"Sure," Annie responded, settling onto the floor with her back to Hunter.

Hunter watched as Annie and Serena started their game. They both looked relaxed and at ease, but he didn't think either was. Annie had spoken of nightmares. Serena had struggled during the past year, too. Losing her brother had been difficult; knowing that he'd been murdered in the line of duty and that his murderer was still on the loose was even harder.

He frowned, pouring himself a cup of coffee. His third of the night. Caffeine overload, but he had a long day to get through. A meeting at headquarters at nine, and then a trip to Steven Antonio's office in the afternoon. The prosecuting attorney was determined to win his case against Saunders and Fiske. He'd been asking for weekly meetings with Annie since her return to St. Louis. Hunter might have to curtail the frequency. She was as prepared for trial as a witness could be, and her safety was paramount.

Hunter glanced at the computer monitor that had been set up on the kitchen counter. The split screen offered views from six security cameras. No sign of trouble outside the apartment building and no sign of it inside. He hadn't expected that there would be. The safe house had been used dozens of times, and it had never been compromised. There was no reason to believe it would be now.

Then again, the little house that they'd been using had never been compromised before, either.

He sipped lukewarm coffee and tried to think of a way that could have happened without someone from the unit being involved. He trusted the men and women he worked with. He depended on them to do their jobs. He'd have trusted any one of them with his life. But someone had leaked Annie's location.

He had to find out who, and he had to do it quickly.

Since Daniel Summers's death, there'd been some tension within the unit. Daniel's murder had left a hole in the team. Josh McCall and Serena felt the loss the most. Serena because Daniel was her brother. Josh because they'd been partners and best friends. There hadn't been much Hunter could do but encourage the team to keep working, keep seeking justice and keep doing exactly what Daniel had always loved. But the newest development in the Delacorte case wasn't going to sit well with anyone. Accusations could be tossed around. That could cause more tension.

No one needed that.

Hunter clenched his fists and walked out of the kitchen. He wasn't used to feeling helpless, but he'd felt helpless when he'd heard about Daniel's murder. He'd promised Serena and himself that he'd find the person responsible, and that he'd make sure that person paid. Over a year later, he still had no leads, no suspects, no clues.

He felt as if he was failing himself and his team.

He would fail them even more if he didn't find the leak and stop it.

Serena and Annie looked up as he entered the room.

"She's beating my socks off," Serena said with

a dramatic sigh. "How about you take the next round, Hunter?"

Not likely. Playing games while he was on duty wasn't something he'd ever done, and he didn't plan to start now. "You're the checker champ, Serena. I'm sure you can take her down if you put your mind to it. I've got to make a couple of calls."

"Are you checking in with the evidence team?" Serena asked.

"Josh was going to do that. I'm going to call him and see if there have been any updates."

Her expression hardened the way it seemed to every time Josh was mentioned. She'd obviously had a problem with him since her brother's murder, and Hunter suspected that she blamed him for Daniel's death.

"Right. I'm sure Josh will know what's going on. Your move, Annie." She turned her attention back to the game.

He could have asked her if she had a problem working with Josh. He didn't because she did her job well. Whatever she might be feeling, she never let it affect her work. That was what mattered.

He walked down the hall and pulled out his cell phone. Joshua's phone rang twice before it jumped to voice mail. He left a brief message asking for information and reminding Josh of their meeting. Hopefully, there would be more information by then.

A quiet sound drifted from Annie's room. Sophia?

She was one of the most well-behaved kids he'd ever met. Quiet and cute, she spent her days toddling around the house and smiling. If he'd had time to be a parent, getting to know Sophia would have convinced him that it was a good idea.

He didn't have time. Not for a wife. Not for kids. Unless he did, he'd never take that step. His siblings had said the same until they'd fallen in love. Now they insisted that he'd change his mind when the right woman came along.

He wasn't sure that would ever happen, because love was never enough to hold a relationship together. There needed to be time, attention, companionship. There needed to be more than a half-hour dinner once a month or a quick phone call between cases.

There needed to be as much commitment to the relationship as there was to work, and Hunter didn't think he'd ever be able to give that. He certainly hadn't had a good example of how to make it work, that was for sure.

He frowned, not sure why he was letting his mind wander in that direction.

Another soft sound drifted from Annie's room. He peeked in the door. The bed was empty. His heart jumped in surprise, but he wasn't worried. No way could Sophia have gone far. Then again, he didn't know how far a toddler would have to go to find trouble in an apartment that wasn't baby-proofed.

"Sophia?" he called as he walked into the room. No answer.

He rounded the bed and found her lying beside it, a blanket clutched in one arm. Still sound asleep by the look of things.

He scooped her up, planning to put her back in bed, but her little arms wrapped round his neck, and she held on tight.

"Time to get back in bed, Sophia," he said.

"Where's Mommy?" She popped her thumb in her mouth and eyed him suspiciously.

"In the living room. She'll be back in a few minutes."

"I want Mommy," she somehow managed to say without taking her thumb out of her mouth.

For such a young kid, she was very articulate, every word she spoke crystal clear. He had good reason to know it. She was speaking more and more lately, her voice high-pitched and sweet. "All right. I'll get her for you."

He tried to put her down again, but she tightened her grip on his neck.

"Hey," he said, easing one of her little arms from his neck before she cut off circulation. "You've got quite a grip, kid."

"I not kid. I Sophia."

The comment surprised a laugh out of him. "Sorry. *Sophia.*"

"Good boy, Hunter," she said solemnly, patting his cheek.

He was more amused than he probably should be. He was working, after all. Protecting Sophia and Annie. He couldn't allow himself to be distracted.

"Come on," he said, carrying her from the room. "Let's get your mom."

"And a cookie?"

He almost laughed again. "That's up to your mom."

"What's up to me?" Annie hurried into the hall. Obviously, she'd heard him talking to Sophia. She took the toddler from his arms and eyed him with the same suspicion he'd seen in her daughter's eyes.

They looked a lot alike. Both with dark hair and big blue eyes. Both with smooth skin and delicate features. Hunter had seen pictures of Joe. His hair had been light brown, his eyes gray. Whatever he'd passed on to his daughter didn't show in her face.

"Sophia wanted a cookie," he said.

"Does Mommy ever give you cookies before breakfast, Sophia?" She looked at her daughter rather than him, and he had the distinct feeling she was trying to cut him out of the conversation, exclude him from their little circle of family.

That should have been just fine. He'd spent the vast majority of his adult years standing on the edges of other people's lives. It was part of the job.

For some reason, with Annie, it bothered him.

With her, the quick pivot and half jog down the hall and away from him was more than annoying. It was downright insulting. He'd been providing for Sophia's needs for months, making sure the little girl was safe and protected. In the last safe house, he'd been the one to buy outlet covers. He'd also been the one to shove them into every outlet in the house so that Sophia wouldn't stick her fingers into the sockets. He'd purchased a car seat for their trips to and from the airport and to and from the prosecuting attorney's office. He'd even researched the best ones, making sure that he bought one with the highest safety rating. He'd purchased cabinet locks for the kitchen and little padded covers for the edges of the coffee table in the living room. Annie hadn't had to think about or worry about any of those things. They'd been done before she'd arrived.

So, yeah, having Sophia snatched from his arms and hurried away as though he might kidnap the kid irked.

He almost asked Annie what her problem was. Why she felt the need to protect her daughter from the guy who'd spent the past month providing everything the little girl needed.

His better self prevailed. His professional self, the one who always kept his cool and never let a witness shake his confidence or his calm, won out over irritation.

Barely.

And that worried him.

Maybe the past year had taken more of a toll than he'd thought it had. Losing Daniel in the line of duty, seeing his team suffer, had given him plenty of sleepless nights. With the Delacorte trial approaching, the danger to Sophia and Annie was intensifying. That had never bothered him with other cases, but this case was different. It involved a completely innocent woman and her child. He'd found himself caring just a little more, going to just a little more trouble for his charges.

Going to a little more trouble was one thing—letting them affect his emotions was another. Once he got Annie safely through the trial, he was going to take a vacation, spend a couple of weeks at his uncle's ranch in Montana. He'd always loved it there. The fresh air and wide-open spaces. The chance to breathe and think without the clutter of city noise and smog.

He glanced at his watch. He needed to be at the office in two hours. His replacement would arrive soon. The best thing he could do was prepare for the meeting.

He grabbed a laptop from the room beside Annie's and carried it into the living room. Annie was in the kitchen, making eggs for Sophia. Serena was manning the monitor.

He settled into a chair, opened the laptop and got to work.

FIVE

The worst thing about being in witness protection in St. Louis was that she was never alone. Ever.

And, sometimes, Annie really wanted to be.

In the six hours she'd been awake, she hadn't had a moment to herself. Serena and Hunter had hovered close by until they'd had to leave for a meeting. After they left, their replacements had done the same.

She rubbed the back of her neck and lifted the blanket Sophia had covered herself with.

"Found you!" she said for the hundredth time.

Sophia giggled and ran away, her chubby legs churning as she zipped past Burke Trier. Tall and muscular with dark hair and eyes, he had a quick smile and an easygoing personality. He was funny, smart and interesting.

He was also a player.

It had taken Annie only a couple of days to figure that out. Not because he'd overstepped any professional lines, but because he constantly seemed to be arriving for his shift after a long night or rushing out because he had a hot date.

His words. Not hers.

Personally, she'd only ever been on nice dates with a nice guy. At least, Joe had *seemed* nice when they'd been dating during high school and college. He had *been* nice, but nice didn't mean honest.

That had been a hard lesson to learn.

She had learned it well. Even if she hadn't, men like Burke had never appealed to her.

She scooped Sophia into her arms, offering Burke an apologetic smile. "She's a little hyper. That seems to happen when she doesn't get enough sleep."

"She's less hyper than my nieces and nephews get when they're tired," he said with the charming smile he used every time they spoke. "She's also pretty steady on her feet. Once all this is over, you should put her in gymnastics or dance or something."

"She's still a little young for that."

"My niece is the same age. My sister-in-law takes her to Mommy and Me classes. Gymnastics and dance."

His sister-in-law obviously had a husband who could help her afford classes. Either that or she had a good job that still allowed her plenty of time to spend with her daughter.

Annie's situation was different.

There was no sense in trying to explain that to Burke. In a few weeks, the trial would be over. She and Sophia would be free to move on. Annie would find a new job and a good day-care center. Hopefully, they'd settle into life and finally start really living again.

"Maybe I'll look into it," she said as she carried Sophia into the kitchen and set her in one of the chairs. "Are you hungry, peanut?"

"For cookies?" Sophia asked. The child loved sweets just like Joe had.

That was one thing she'd gotten from her father.

"For lunch, silly," she responded, forcing some cheerfulness into her voice. Sophia deserved more than a mother who constantly bemoaned her fate. "But you *can* have a cookie when you're finished."

"Yay!" Sophia clapped her hands, her little eyes barely above the rim of the table. She needed a booster seat, but Annie didn't want to ask. It seemed as if all she did was ask for things. Hunter had assured her that it was his team's job to make her and Sophia comfortable, but she was starting to feel like a bird in a cage. Given everything she needed, but denied the freedom she craved.

"I'll bring a high chair for her tomorrow," Burke offered, his attention on the computer monitor set up on the counter.

"That's okay. We're only going to be here a few more weeks."

"A few weeks is a long time for a little girl." He pulled a phone from his pocket and typed something into it. "There. Sent myself a text, and I sent one to Hunter. Between the two of us, we'll get it done."

"Really, Burke—"

His cell phone rang, and he raised a hand.

"It's Hunter. Hold that thought, okay?" He made it sound as though they'd been having an intimate conversation, a man and a woman in the middle of something more than a discussion about booster seats. Or maybe that was just what she heard because Joe had said the same thing to her so many times.

Hold that thought, sweetie. I need to take this call.

Hang on to that thought for a minute. My boss is calling me.

She'd never doubted that she was being interrupted for a good cause. She'd always waited patiently, and then continued the conversation as if the interruption hadn't happened.

Her throat felt tight and her eyes burned, but she'd cried every tear she could in the weeks after Joe's death.

She pulled cheese out of the refrigerator, broke it into a few small pieces and put them on a plate. There was a package of crackers on the counter. She put a couple on the plate. Not much of a lunch, but Sophia tended to graze more than eat.

"Here you go, Sophia." She set the plate in front of her daughter, trying hard not to eavesdrop on the conversation Burke was having. It was hard not to, though. Especially since the conversation seemed to be about her.

"Okay," he said, meeting her eyes and smiling. "I'll let her know." He shoved the phone in his pocket, took a couple of crackers from the open package. "Your meeting with Antonio has been pushed forward. Hunter will be here in twenty minutes to pick you up."

Twenty minutes would have been plenty of time if she'd had clean clothes for herself and Sophia. A brush would have been nice, too.

"I'm not exactly dressed for a meeting," she said, glancing down at the sweatshirt and jeans she'd been wearing for the better part of two days.

"Did you check the drawers and closet in your room? Usually, we keep a few things stocked. Just in case we have an emergency like this."

"I'll check, but Sophia needs some things, too. All her clothes are back at the house."

"I'll have Serena pick them up on her way back here tonight. At least, I'll ask her to. Knowing her, she already has that on her schedule for the day."

"Thanks, Burke. Let's get ready to go," she said, ready to scoop Sophia into her arms.

"Actually—" Burke put a hand on her arm "—Hunter thinks it would be best if she stays here."

"I don't really care what Hunter thinks." At least,

she didn't care much what he thought when it came to raising her daughter.

"He's worried about what happened last night, Annie."

"He's been worried since the day I met him, and he was probably worried long before that," she pointed out.

"That's what makes him good at his job. He takes it seriously. He thinks about every detail, and he plans for every eventuality. If he's worried about Sophia being out today, you'd be wise to be worried, too." There was an edge to his voice that Annie hadn't heard before, a seriousness to his eyes that she couldn't ignore.

"I'll..." She glanced at Sophia. She was happily munching on a cracker and smashing a piece of cheese between her fingers. Annie hated to go anywhere without her. Usually, Hunter was happy to accommodate that. The fact that he wasn't this time made her uneasy. "...talk to Hunter when he gets here."

"You can talk all you want, but the plans are set. I'm going to stay here with Sophia. Hunter and Serena are going to escort you to the attorney's office."

"I really don't feel comfortable leaving her here, Burke," she tried to protest.

"You don't trust me to watch your daughter?"

"It's not that."

"Then what is it?"

"I just don't really like leaving her when I go out." Mostly because no matter how hard she tried, she couldn't forget the feeling of returning home to a wounded husband and a missing baby. She didn't want to ever have to live through that again. "Besides, the apartment isn't toddler-proof. She could get into all kinds of trouble while I'm gone."

"You know that fifty years ago people didn't believe in childproofing, right? I mean, they didn't have all the little gadgets to keep kids from putting their fingers into sockets or pulling furniture over on themselves."

"And?"

"Most kids lived," he said drily. "And I'm pretty sure that if I can watch my brother's identical twins for an entire weekend, I can watch Sophia for a couple of hours."

"But—"

"Look, Annie," he cut in. "We try to be accommodating, but when it comes to the safety of the people we're protecting, we don't believe in taking chances. If you don't hurry and get ready, you're going to be late for your appointment."

He turned his attention back to the computer monitor. Apparently, he was done with their conversation.

Annie didn't really want to be done. She didn't want to go to the meeting dressed in clothes she'd slept in, either. She carried Sophia into the room and set her down. Since Joe died, she'd had to leave Sophia with sitters so that she could work. It had taken a while, but she'd gotten used to that. Still, St. Louis was the city where everything had gone wrong. It was the place where she'd lost every dream she'd ever dreamed, and the place where she'd been forced to grow up, become a stronger person, a better one. That was the good that had come out of the bad.

When she was really feeling down, she tried to remember it.

"Okay, Sophia," she said. "Mommy has to go out for a while. Want to help me pick something to wear?" She opened a dresser drawer. Jeans in a variety of sizes. Another drawer had T-shirts and sweatshirts. Nothing she'd have chosen for a business meeting.

Not that this was business exactly.

She grabbed what she needed and hurried into the bathroom. She'd perfected the art of quick showers and quick changes when Sophia was younger. There was no blow-dryer, so she toweled her hair dry and brushed it while Sophia sang her version of "Jingle Bells."

"Christmas is over, sweetie. How about you sing something different?" she suggested as she walked out of the bathroom.

Sophia followed, standing close as Annie eyed herself in the dresser mirror. The jeans were dark, straight and a little loose, the T-shirt tighter than she normally wore. At least it was dark, the hem falling to her hips. She looked almost put together. Even with her hair only half-dry and no makeup on her face.

Voices drifted into the room. Hunter and Serena must have returned.

She had to get going, but she still wasn't happy about leaving Sophia. There wasn't much for a two-year-old to do in the apartment. No books. No toys. The few things Sophia had gotten for Christmas had been left behind when they'd run from the former safe house.

"Come on, Sophia. Let's go." She walked out into the hall, following the sounds of voices into the kitchen. Four people were there. Hunter. Serena. Burke. Joshua McCall.

Serena didn't look happy, and the tension in the room was so thick Annie could have cut it with a knife.

"Ready?" Hunter asked. *He* didn't seem upset or tense. His hands were relaxed, his expression neutral.

It was what she'd come to expect of him. He never seemed fazed by anything. Calm, cool, efficient. She couldn't have asked for more from a bodyguard, so she couldn't complain.

Sometimes, though, she had the absurd urge to rattle his cage just to see what would happen.

Must be boredom rearing its ugly head.

"Yes, but I was thinking that Sophia could come with us. This is a new place and—"

"I'm sorry, Annie. That's out of the question. After last night, we can't be too careful. There will be less risk for everyone if we leave Sophia here."

She could have argued, but she'd known Hunter long enough to know it would be a waste of time. "How long will we be gone?"

"A couple of hours. Burke and I are going to escort you. Josh and Serena will stay here. Sophia will be in good hands."

"I thought Burke was—" Serena began.

"We've already discussed it," Josh cut in, his words curt, his expression neutral. Whatever they'd discussed, he didn't seem very happy about the outcome.

Not Annie's business. All she had to worry about was getting to the attorney's office and getting back to Sophia. The sooner the better.

"Give Mommy a kiss, Sophia," she said, crouching down and opening her arms.

Sophia ran into them, her soft hair brushing Annie's chin. She smelled like baby shampoo and crackers, and Annie's heart ached with the depth of the love she felt for her.

"Be good for Serena and Josh, okay?" she said.

"No," Sophia responded.

Burke laughed. "Glad I got voted out of staying with you, then, kid."

No one else seemed amused.

"Of course you'll be good," Annie said hurriedly. Sophia never caused problems. At least, that was what her babysitter in Milwaukee said.

"She'll be as good as gold. You go on and get through the meeting. The trial is coming up soon, and we want you as prepared as possible." Josh lifted Sophia and tickled her belly.

"He's right. We can't miss this appointment." Hunter cupped Annie's elbow and urged her to the door, hoping she wasn't going to continue arguing. The change in meeting time hadn't thrilled him, but it was his job to work with the prosecuting attorney's office. He accommodated their schedule. Not the other way around.

He glanced at his watch. They were already running late.

"Everything is clear on the security cameras," Serena announced, her voice as tight and hard as her expression. She wasn't happy about babysitting duty, but Hunter had thought Annie would be more comfortable having a woman babysit her daughter.

From the look on her face, he'd say she wouldn't be comfortable with *anyone* babysitting.

He could understand that. Family was important. More important than jobs or obligations. Certainly more important than meetings with lawyers who'd already been met with.

Annie didn't say a word as he led her into the hall.

Not one complaint or protest. Pretty typical, and fairly unusual for the people he worked with. Most of them had truckloads of complaints and hour-long protest sessions.

Burke stepped into the elevator ahead of them, holding the door as Annie stepped in. Hunter didn't miss Burke's quick assessing glance or the way his eyes lingered on Annie's hair or her tight black T-shirt. Not surprising. Even in baggy jeans and a T-shirt, her hair damp and no makeup on her face, she was beautiful. Burke loved beautiful women, and he pursued them with a shocking amount of zeal. No deep emotions about any breakups. No mourning over lost love. Just one relationship after another. If not for the fact that Annie was a client that they were protecting, Hunter was sure Burke would be pursuing her.

If Annie noticed Burke's attention, she didn't let on.

"Are you sure this is only going to take a couple of hours?" she asked, her blue eyes shadowed from lack of sleep, her face just a little too pale. A strand of dark hair fell across her cheek, and Hunter clenched his fist to keep from brushing it back.

"I'd like to say I was," he responded as the elevator door closed. "But you know how these things go."

"The last meeting lasted five hours, and most of

it, I wasn't even involved in." She ran her fingers through her hair in a quick impatient gesture.

"It shouldn't be as long today," Burke offered before Hunter could respond. He smiled the charming smile that seemed to win him a new girlfriend every week.

Hunter had no interest in winning anything but Annie's cooperation. The smile still annoyed him. Maybe he needed to have a talk with Burke about professionalism. *After* they got Annie where she needed to be and back safely.

The elevator door slid open, and Burke stepped out first, speaking quietly into his radio. Either Serena or Josh would be manning the computer, watching for any trouble on the security cameras.

There'd been nothing to indicate that Annie's safety had been compromised again, but they couldn't afford to take any chances. Adrenaline pulsed through Hunter's blood as he led her across the parking lot. Burke already had the car door open, his gaze scanning the area.

"Straight into the car," Hunter murmured in Annie's ear, the scent of shampoo and soap drifting on the cold afternoon air.

She was halfway in the car when the world exploded, the sound reverberating through the lot, the force of the blast slamming Hunter to his knees. He fell into Annie, knocking her farther into the car.

"Move!" he shouted, shoving her inside and crawling in behind her.

Flames poured from a car near the edge of the lot. Sirens blared. Water poured from ceiling sprinklers.

Someone had planned it all, and if Hunter and Burke weren't careful, that person would get the shot at Annie he wanted.

"Back or front exit?" Burke asked as Hunter slammed the door shut.

He surveyed the parking garage quickly. Back entrance clear of fire. Front entrance smoke and flame-filled.

There was only one choice, and he made it.

"Front," he growled.

SIX

Flames.

Smoke.

Water pouring from the sky.

People streaming from the building, confusion on their faces. All of it whizzing by as the car zipped toward the exit.

Sophia!

Annie scrambled for the door handle, desperate to get out of the car. She had to get to Sophia, had to make sure she was okay.

"What are you doing?" Hunter shouted, dragging her back across the seat, his arm a steel band around her waist.

She clawed at his hand, tried to pry his fingers from her waist. "Sophia! I have to get to her."

"By getting yourself killed?" he shouted.

"She needs me."

"Alive, and you won't be if you jump out of the car." His grip didn't loosen as Burke sped out of the parking garage. "Everything is under control,

Annie. I promise you that, but it won't be if you don't start cooperating."

"*Start* cooperating? All I've done for a year is follow your rules and protocols and suggestions." And she was done. She wanted out of the car, out of witness protection, out of the situation she was in. She wanted to get her daughter and go home.

Wherever home was.

Not St. Louis. Not anymore.

Not Milwaukee, either.

Somewhere where she could start over, make a good, peaceful and safe life.

All she had to do was get to Sophia.

She shoved his arm again, but it was rock solid, his palm pressed tight against her side. "Let me go," she muttered.

"Not until you agree that you're not going to jump out of this car."

She pressed her lips together. The car was picking up speed, buildings flying by in her periphery. If she didn't break her neck hitting the pavement, she'd probably be run over by an oncoming vehicle. She looked over her shoulder, saw clouds of smoke billowing from the parking garage.

Everyone would have to be evacuated. The structure couldn't be stable. Was Sophia still inside the building? Outside it? "You can't hold me against my will. It's kidnapping. Pull over and let me out."

"Where would you go? Back to the building where someone is probably waiting to kill you?"

"Back for my daughter."

"She's not there. Josh and Serena have already evacuated. They're on their way to headquarters. We'll meet them there."

The truth or a lie?

She wouldn't put it past Hunter to say whatever was necessary to get her to cooperate. He'd never think of it as being dishonest because he'd believe it was for the greater good.

She glanced at the apartment again. People stood on the sidewalk, staring at the flames that licked the outside wall of the structure.

Was someone standing in the crowd, waiting for her to emerge? She'd be an idiot to go back if Sophia was safe. She sagged against Hunter, her muscles loose with fear.

"That's better," Hunter murmured in her ear, his arm slipping from her waist. He smelled like soap and sunshine, his warmth seeping through her coat and jeans, seeping into her skin and bones until she wanted to melt against him and beg him to tell her everything was going to be okay.

She scooted back across the car, her heart thumping painfully.

She could not melt for anyone. Couldn't give in to her neediness. That was what had gotten her into trouble before. That and her too-trusting nature.

She shifted in her seat, looking out the back window. A block from the apartment building, and she could smell the acrid smoke. More people stood on the sidewalk, the growing crowds pressing in toward one another, a writhing mass of humanity all vying for the best view of the burning garage. A man separated himself from the crowd, a little girl in his arms. Her dark hair glinted in the sunlight, the curls bouncing as the man moved.

Sophia!

Annie would know her daughter anywhere from any distance.

Hunter *had* lied.

Sophia wasn't safe. She was standing outside the apartment complex in Josh McCall's arms.

She'd been angry before. Angry with Joe when bills hadn't been paid. Angrier when she'd found out about his lies and the debt he'd accrued.

Up until that moment, though, she'd never been furious. Never been so angry that her head hurt and her lungs ached and she wanted to scream until her throat was raw.

She watched as Josh stepped to the curb and looked up the street. Sophia waved at the passing cars, oblivious to the danger she was in. Oblivious to the smoke and people and chaos.

Hunter said something, but the words didn't register.

She shifted in her seat, cold with fury and with fear.

The car slowed as it neared a busy intersection, the red light ahead stopping the cars in front of them.

Burke slowed the car to a crawl but didn't stop completely.

The light turned green, and she knew it was now or never. She could sit like a lump and do what she'd been told, or she could go get her daughter and run as far and as fast as she'd ever run in her life.

She grabbed the door handle, yanked it open and jumped.

She hit the ground hard, tumbling onto her hands and knees. She was up before any pain registered, running back toward the apartment and her daughter, dodging people and a bicycle.

Someone shouted her name.

She ignored it, her gaze on Sophia and Josh.

A car pulled to the curb in front of them, the door swinging open.

"Wait!" she shouted.

Josh glanced her way, his eyes widening.

He didn't pause, though, didn't alter whatever plan he was part of. He climbed into the car and closed the door.

Someone snagged the back of Annie's coat and yanked her backward. She fell into a hard chest and harder arms.

"This is the stupidest thing I have ever seen anyone do," Hunter growled.

"You lied to me!" she retorted, swinging around so they were face-to-face. He was taller, bigger and more intimidating, but she had righteous anger on her side.

"Now isn't the time to discuss it."

"Now is the only time I'm going to discuss anything with you ever again. I want my daughter. I want—"

"To be shot dead on the sidewalk in St. Louis?" His gaze was as cold as his words, his eyes icy and hard. "Because that could happen, Annie. What do you think that bomb was? Some coincidental misfortune?"

He dragged her to the curb as a car pulled up.

Black and new-looking. The same one Josh had gotten into.

The door swung open, and Josh reached for her arm, yanking her into the car so quickly she didn't have time to think about what was happening. The door slammed shut. The car took off.

"Mommy!" Sophia squealed from her car seat, her eyes bright with excitement, her curly hair bouncing with joy.

She looked fine.

She looked better than fine. She looked cared for and safe.

Josh, on the other hand, looked fit to be tied.

"That," he said, "was the rashest thing I have ever seen anyone do in the ten years I've been working for the marshals."

"Rash but brave," Serena said as she steered the

car onto a side street and headed for the interstate. "You still shouldn't have done it. Anyone could have been out there with a gun. One bullet. That's all it would have taken."

That was all it had taken to steal Joe's life.

One bullet through the chest. He'd bled to death before the ambulance had arrived.

Annie shuddered. Her knees and palms throbbed, her head ached, and all the rage that had fed her escape was gone.

All she felt was tired.

But she'd felt that way for a year.

Sophia reached for her.

"Hey, sweetie," she said, taking her daughter's hand. She'd do anything for Sophia. Even risk her life, but Sophia was safe, had been safe. Just like Hunter had said.

She owed him an apology.

She owed everyone an apology, but her throat was too clogged with regret to offer it. She looked out the window instead, wishing she were anywhere else but sitting in a car heading to U.S. Marshals headquarters.

Hunter didn't lose his temper often, but he'd been pushed past the point of being reasonable. Behind him the fire had been doused by the sprinkler system, the smoke slowly dissipating. Whoever had planted the bomb hadn't meant to take out the building. He'd meant to take out Annie. A distraction was the perfect cover for swift and covert movement.

Hunter had no doubt that the perp was still near the building. Probably around the back where more people were gathered. If he'd been at the front of the building when Annie had jumped from the car...

He clenched his teeth. Counted to a hundred.

Told himself that he wasn't going to lay into Annie the minute he saw her.

Burke finally managed to navigate back to the building, his dark sedan moving slowly through the thickening traffic. Sirens were blaring and news trucks were bottlenecking the side streets.

In other circumstances, Hunter would have stuck around to help process the crime scene, but he needed to get back to headquarters. Somehow, the safe house had been found. Again.

Burke pulled up to the curb, and Hunter climbed into the car.

"We're meeting Josh and Serena at headquarters. I've already called Antonio," he growled. "If he wants to see Annie, he can do it there."

"Sounds like a plan," Burke responded. "Provided Annie doesn't decide to jump out of Serena's car."

"I think she's done for the day. Now that she's with her daughter, she should stay put."

"Or take Sophia and run. It's what I'd do if I were in her shoes."

"Then let's both thank God she's not you," Hunter muttered, the thought of Annie taking Sophia and leaving town chilling his blood. No way could he protect either of them if she did that.

"She surprised me, I'll tell you that," Burke continued as if Hunter hadn't spoken. He didn't sound nearly as upset as Hunter. "I didn't think she had it in her to buck the system."

"Me neither. Obviously, we were both wrong."

"You sound like you want to wring her neck."

"I want to get it through her head that we have things under control. Her daughter was never in harm's way, and she won't be as long as Annie follows the rules."

"If that were your kid, would you be so quick to think that a bunch of strangers could keep her safe?" Burke asked as he merged onto the interstate.

"What does that have to do with anything?" Hunter responded, frustrated with the question and the conversation.

"The way I see it, a parent is supposed to do anything for her child. Including jumping from a moving vehicle."

"And risking having her head blown off?"

"I'd do it if I had a kid," Burke said simply.

Hunter would, too.

Knowing it stole some of his anger.

"All right. I get your point, but she's the key witness in the case against Saunders and Fiske. We lose her, and they might lose the case."

"And that would be bad for your reputation?"

"It would be bad for justice, Burke," Hunter responded drily. He knew he had a reputation as cold and unfeeling, but he didn't always like it.

"It was a joke, Hunter. I know you well enough to know you care. I care, too, but that doesn't seem to be doing Annie any good. We've had her at two safe houses, and she's been found both times."

"Which means that someone is leaking information to friends of Fiske and Saunders."

"Exactly what I've been thinking."

"I trust our team, Burke. I can't believe anyone on it would betray us." He didn't *want* to believe it. Maybe he didn't have to. Administrative staff could access information from the main database at the office.

"It could be anyone at the office." Burke echoed Hunter's thoughts. "We need to get some computer forensic guys in. If someone tapped into the computer databases, they'll know it."

"We'll make the call when we get to the office," Hunter agreed. "We also need to find a place where Annie and her daughter will be safe until the trial."

"So far, we're batting a thousand on that."

"We could move them out of state again until the trial."

"Or we could keep them even closer to home than they've already been. Somewhere we both spend time, so that no one at the office will think anything about us being there." Burke tapped his fingers on the steering wheel.

"I don't think the office is baby-friendly, Burke."

"Not the office. Our place."

"No." Hunter didn't even have to think about the answer. The rental they shared was plenty big enough for a large family, but it wasn't approved as a safe house. Even if it was, having the Delacortes stay there wouldn't work.

"Why not?"

"This isn't personal, Burke. It's professional."

"That makes the plan even better."

"What plan?" Hunter was used to Burke's out-of-the-box thinking. The guy had a habit of skirting rules and flying by the seat of his pants. Usually it worked out well for him, but that didn't mean Hunter approved of his methods.

"We take the Delacortes to our place. Under the radar. No one knows they're there except for our team. We'll run shifts. Me, you, Josh and Serena. No one else included. That will minimize the chance of Annie being found again."

Hunter's knee-jerk reaction was to say no again, but, so far, playing by the book hadn't worked. Maybe they did need to switch things up, try something different. "That will mean almost no time off for any of us. You realize that, right?"

"It's only for a couple of weeks. I don't know about everyone else, but I could use the extra pay."

"Dating is bleeding you dry, huh?"

Burke's hands tightened on the steering wheel, and something flashed across his face. It could have been anger or sorrow.

"Nah. I just have some expenses coming up," he said, all of his normal animation gone.

"Is it anything I can help with?"

"No, but if that changes, I'll let you know."

Hunter respected his friend too much to push for more information, so he let it go. "We'll have to check with the rest of the team. If they agree, that might be the direction we take."

"I'm not sure there's another direction we can go," Burke said.

He could have been right, but Hunter never made impulsive decisions, and he didn't move forward with plans until he had confidence that they'd work out.

This one might if they could keep Annie's location secret, and if he could keep himself from getting even more involved in her life than he already was.

That was the real problem with the plan. Nothing about protocol or rules. There was just something about Annie. Something different, and that might prove to be dangerous to Hunter's professionalism and his heart.

He couldn't risk either one.

SEVEN

It took only twenty minutes to reach U.S. Marshals headquarters. Annie would have preferred twenty hours. Maybe even twenty days.

She braced herself as Serena pulled up to the tall brick building. No doubt, Hunter was on his way. She really didn't want to face him again. There wasn't anything she could say that would excuse what she'd done, and she couldn't promise that she wouldn't do the same thing again.

Sophia would always be first. Annie didn't know any other way to do things.

"Let's get her out of her car seat and get both of you inside," Josh said. He sounded tired.

She *felt* tired, her body heavy as she unhooked Sophia's straps and lifted her from the seat.

They were as close to the door as Serena could get, but Annie still felt nervous as she followed Josh out of the car. Two steps, and she was inside the building and walking through a wide foyer.

"We've got a room ready for you and Serena upstairs." Josh punched the elevator button and the doors opened.

"How long will we be here?" Not that it mattered. She'd stay as long as they wanted her to, leave when they told her to, go where they brought her.

It had been that way for a year.

She hadn't complained because she'd agreed to cooperate with the marshals. She'd listened to Hunter's list of rules and regulations, and she'd followed every one of them. That had seemed like the only way to protect Sophia.

She stepped into the elevator, nearly falling over as Sophia reached for the buttons. "I push!" she said.

"Not this time, sweetie. Let Mr. Josh do it."

"She can. Fourth floor."

"Hold the elevator!" Serena called as she jogged toward them.

She wasn't alone.

Hunter and Burke were just a few feet behind her.

Great. They'd all be on the elevator together. Smashed together like sardines.

Okay. Maybe not that bad, but it would be awkward.

Very awkward considering that less than an hour ago, Hunter had been ready to take Annie's head off.

Josh held the door, and all three crowded in.

Perfect.

No one spoke, the short ride to the fourth floor dead silent.

As soon as the doors opened, everyone filed out.

She was last, Sophia reaching for Hunter as she stepped into a long corridor.

"Hold me!" she demanded.

"No, Sophia. Mr. Hunter is busy," Annie told her, her heart racing as Hunter's dark gaze came to rest on her face. He didn't look happy.

"We're heading to the same place, so I guess I'm not so busy that I can't carry her there," he said dispassionately. All his anger seemed to be gone, any remnant well hidden beneath his calm facade. "Come on, Sophia. You want some juice?"

"Juice," she agreed happily, squealing with delight as he lifted her to his shoulders. She clutched his hair with both fists as he walked down the hall.

They looked cute together. If Annie hadn't known better, she'd have thought they were father and daughter. The thought hurt way down deep where all her dreams of a happy family had lived before Joe had died.

She followed them to a room at the end of the hall. Hunter opened the door, set Sophia down. "Stay here with your mommy. I'm going to get some juice."

He stepped back, gestured for Annie to enter.

Not a word to her. No warning. No caution. Nothing.

Despite his calmness, she was pretty certain he was still upset.

She walked into the room, had barely cleared the

threshold when he closed the door. He didn't slam it, but she heard the soft click of a lock.

Her heart jumped, and she turned the knob.

He *had* locked her in!

She almost couldn't believe it. In the year she'd known him, in the months that she'd spent with him as her primary contact with the world, she'd never known him to be anything other reasonable.

Locking someone into a room didn't seem reasonable.

Unless you don't trust that person to stay put.

The thought whispered through her mind. She couldn't deny it. She couldn't deny that she'd earned his distrust, either. No matter her reasons, she'd put herself and Hunter's team in danger.

She took Sophia's hand and walked to a table that sat in the middle of the room. Conference length and surrounded by chairs, it had probably been used dozens of times by the men and women who were guarding her. There was nothing else in the room. No computers. No televisions. No scraps of paper. She didn't even see a trash can.

Tall windows stretched the length of one wall and looked out onto the parking lot. None of them opened. She tried the door handle again. Still locked. She'd known it would be, but in all the time she'd been in the witness protection program, she'd never felt like a prisoner.

Now she did.

She didn't like it.

She settled into a chair, watching as Sophia toddled around the room. Happy as a lark, not a care in the world. That was what Annie had wanted. From the very beginning, her goal had been to seek justice for Joe and to keep Sophia safe and free of danger.

The doorknob rattled and the door opened.

Her heart jumped in anticipation, her muscles tensed.

Josh walked into the room and she nearly sagged with relief. As much as she wanted out of the locked room, she didn't want to face Hunter again. Not until she knew her emotions were completely under control.

"Juice for the kid." Josh held up a juice box. "And diet soda for her mother."

"Thanks."

"Thank Hunter when you see him. He bought both from the vending machine."

"Where is he?" she asked, even though she told herself she didn't want or need to know.

"Meeting with the rest of the team. I have to get back. Make yourself as comfortable as you can. I don't know how long we'll be." He walked out into the hall, closed the door and locked it.

Probably on orders from Hunter.

"Boo-boo, Mommy?" Sophia asked, poking at Annie's raw knee. All the skin had been scraped off, blood still seeping from a deep gash.

"Yes." She glanced around the room. Nothing to staunch the flow of blood. Not that she was going to bleed to death from the wound. The other knee was just as raw. Both palms were ripped to shreds, too.

"You know what, Sophia? Your mom is an idiot," she muttered.

An idiot who wanted out of witness protection.

She didn't know if she'd get that, though.

She'd agreed to testify, and if she didn't…then what? She'd be on her own, starting over in a new town and hoping that whoever had been tracking her down in St. Louis would leave her alone once the trial was over.

Even if he did, she didn't know if she could live with her decision. Running sounded like a good plan, but if the men who'd killed Joe got off because she didn't testify…

The lock clicked and the door swung open.

Every muscle in her body tensed as Hunter strode into the room.

"Okay, we have a new plan. It's going to keep you safe as long as you cooperate," he said.

No preamble. No niceties. But that was Hunter. Blunt and to the point.

"You've said that before."

"And I meant it before. I've never had this kind of trouble keeping a witness hidden. I'm not planning on ever having this kind of trouble again."

"Sounds good, but I was thinking—"

"Hunt!" Sophia squealed, holding her arms up to Hunter. He picked her up, letting her pat his cheeks and tug on his hair.

"Go ahead, Annie. Tell me what you were thinking," he said. "That you'd cut out before the trial? Maybe make a new life somewhere? That you'd be better off trying to protect Sophia yourself than relying on us to do it for you?"

Yes. Yes. And yes.

She didn't want to admit it, though, because she didn't want him to know how accurately he'd read her.

"I was thinking that, until today, I've done nothing but cooperate. It hasn't done me any good."

"It's kept you alive." His gaze dropped to her legs, and he touched the ripped edge of her jeans. She felt the warmth of his finger, the quick zip of awareness that arced between them. "But it didn't keep you from getting hurt. Wait here. I'll be right back," Hunter said, his hand dropping away.

He hurried out of the room, and she could breathe again.

She couldn't deny what he'd said. Being in witness protection had kept her alive, but she wasn't sure it had kept her safe. She didn't *feel* safe. That was for sure. And that was what she wanted. To feel safe. To know that she was doing everything she could to make sure Sophia was okay. She'd promised Joe. Promised him as he took his final breath because Sophia had been his last thought, his only thought as he lay dying.

Don't let anything happen to the baby.

His words had set the thought in Annie's head that something *could* happen to their little girl. She didn't believe in premonitions, but at night, when she couldn't sleep, she wondered if Joe might have had some hint of the future during his dying minutes.

Wondered and worried.

Even though she knew that God was in control, even though she'd always trusted Him, she hadn't been able to shake the anxiety that had plagued her since Joe's death.

She settled into a chair and watched Sophia run from one end of the room to the other. She had a lot of energy. Just like her father. She also had limitless amounts of joy and enthusiasm. Two more traits that she shared with Joe.

Sometimes, it was hard to think about that. Hard to acknowledge how similar Sophia's personality was to her father's.

"You'll do better than your daddy, though, won't you, sweetie?" she said as Sophia ran toward her.

"Juice?" Sophia asked, resting her hands on Annie's thighs and looking up into her face.

"How about we wait until later?"

"Wait for what?" Hunter stepped back into the room, a small white first-aid kit in his hands.

"She wants more juice."

"She's probably hungry, too," he said. "We can get her something to eat once we're finished here."

"I thought we *were* finished." She stood, wincing as her knees straightened.

"Almost." He opened the first-aid kit and took out packets of alcohol wipes. "Go ahead and sit down again."

"What—?"

"We're both tired, Annie. How about you just do what I'm asking, so we don't have to argue about it?"

"Fine." She dropped into the chair, bracing herself as he opened one of the packets. "But I can do that—"

"Too late." He snagged her left calf, holding her leg still as he swiped at her knee. She hissed, all the air seeping out of her lungs.

"That hurts!"

"I'm sure it does." He didn't stop, and she couldn't scoot back far enough to get away from his hands.

"I help!" Sophia yelled, grabbing one of the wipes.

"Not yet, Sophia," Hunter said gently. "You can help with the Band-Aids."

He took the wipe from her hand and pulled his cell phone out of his pocket.

"Here. You can hold this for me." He handed the phone to the toddler, and Sophia pressed it to her ear. Obviously, the kid knew exactly what to do with a phone.

"I'm not sure letting her play with that is the best idea, Hunter," Annie said. "She's only two."

"It's turned off."

"She could break it." She winced as he dabbed antibiotic ointment onto her knee.

"If she does, I'll get a new one." He didn't seem at all concerned. That didn't surprise Annie. In every other way, he'd seemed cold and unfeeling, but when it came to Sophia, he was warm and caring.

He'd make a good father.

Maybe he *was* a good father.

She'd never thought to ask. Never really thought much about what his life was like outside work because he'd always seemed so devoted to his job, so completely driven by his need to follow the rules and maintain protocol.

"Do you have children?" The question slipped out as he opened a large gauze pad and pressed it to her knee.

He stilled, his palm pressed to her knee, his fingers warm on her lower thigh. She could feel the pad of each digit, the heat of his palm. Her skin tingled in response. She inhaled sharply, her heart pounding way too fast.

"No," Hunter finally said, smiling a little as he met her eyes. "My life is too busy for a family."

"That's sad." It really was. A guy like Hunter should have a wife and kids to care for.

"Why do you say that?" He taped down the gauze and moved on to the next knee. This one was worse, a deep cut still oozing blood onto her ripped jeans.

"You're putting all your energy into strangers. Why not put it into people you love?"

"Because my job requires all my energy, and if I had a family, one or the other would suffer. I'm not willing for that to happen." He pressed a piece of folded gauze to her oozing knee.

"Ouch!"

"Sorry."

"You don't sound sorry." He didn't. He sounded annoyed. She wasn't sure if it was because of her question or because he was taking precious time to clean wounds that she'd caused.

"I am, but I'd be sorrier if I weren't thinking about how you did this to yourself and about how I let you." He lifted the gauze and eyed the cut. "Still bleeding."

"It'll stop. Just stick the gauze on and let's get out of here." She took gauze from the first-aid kit, slapped tape on both sides of it and brushed his hand away.

She pressed the gauze to her knee, not even bothering to center it over the cut. She didn't want to have a conversation about her actions. She couldn't explain them. Not in any way that she thought Hunter would understand.

"There. Done." She stood.

"Not quite." He grabbed her wrist, tugging her to a stop.

"Wh—"

He flipped her hand over, frowning at the raw skin on her palm. "This is going to hurt for a few days."

"I'll live."

"Let's hope so," he muttered, swabbing her hand with alcohol.

It stung like crazy, but she refused to complain. He was right. She'd done this to herself.

"You know," she said as he studied her other palm, "you didn't let me do this, Hunter. I did it all by myself."

"I don't agree. Neither do my coworkers."

She hadn't thought about how her escape might be viewed by the men and women who worked for Hunter. She'd known before she'd met him that he had a great reputation within the marshals. The FBI agents and prosecuting attorney that she'd met with after Joe's death had assured her that the best of the best would be protecting her and making sure she made it to trial safely.

Her escape had probably embarrassed Hunter, and she hated that. The last thing she ever wanted to do was hurt someone.

"Sometimes I do things without thinking them through," she admitted.

"I guess that makes you human." He finished cleaning her palms and tossed wrappers and gauze onto the table. "How about we just move on from here?"

"So, forgive and forget?"

"More like forgive and remember so that we can learn from our mistakes." He smiled a little as he answered, his eyes the deep black of a moonless night. They were darker than she'd thought, the irises rimmed with black, his lashes thick and long.

A handsome man. Really handsome, and she wasn't quite sure why it had taken her so long to notice.

She looked away, saw that Sophia had snatched several Band-Aids from the first-aid kit.

It was as good a distraction as any.

She took them and spent a little too much time neatly organizing the box.

Hunter didn't say a word, but she could feel the weight of his stare, feel the warmth of his body as he moved closer.

"You can't avoid it forever," he said quietly.

"What?" Did he know that she had been avoiding his eyes, his handsome face, the butterflies that were fluttering in her stomach?

"Hearing the new plan and agreeing to it."

"Okay." Relieved, she closed the first-aid kit, met his eyes. "Go ahead. Tell me all about it."

EIGHT

"Are you kidding me?" Annie said so loudly that Hunter was pretty sure the windowpanes shook. "That is the worst plan I've ever heard!"

He'd had a feeling she would react that way when he'd told her that he planned to bring her to the house he shared with Burke.

Truth be told, he wasn't all that happy with the plan, either, but after discussing it with the team, he'd had to agree that it was the best option for keeping Annie safe.

"I disagree. The worst plan would be me putting you into another safe house."

"Actually," she said, lifting Sophia into her arms and heading toward the door. "The worst plan would be me sticking around and hoping that you guys can still do what you promised me that you would."

"What's that supposed to mean?"

"Forget the meeting with Antonio. Forget the whole thing! I'm getting out of here." The meeting with Antonio had been postponed until they got

Annie settled, but Hunter didn't think now was the right time to tell her that. "Where are you going?"

"I don't know." She tossed the words over her shoulder as she walked into the hall.

He followed, but he didn't try to stop her.

Let her go and see how far she could get with no transportation and no money.

Not far. That was for sure. She didn't even have a purse. No identification. Not a cent on her that Hunter knew about. And when it came to Annie, he knew just about everything.

She made it all the way down to the lobby before she realized how desperate her situation was. Outside, sunlight splashed across the parking lot, dark clouds dotting the horizon. The day was waning, and he was tired, but he'd shadow her for as long as it took for her to realize that she had no choice but to keep cooperating.

She paused at the double doors, peering out into the parking lot as if she might be able to see any threat that might be waiting for her there.

"You don't have any money," he pointed out, figuring that she might need a little more incentive for sticking around. "Or a vehicle. No clothes for Sophia. No diapers. No food."

The muscles in her back tensed.

"You don't have anywhere to go, either. Even if you had a cell phone and could make a phone call, would you want to put family or friends at risk?"

He hammered the last nail into the coffin, and her shoulders sagged.

"I'm not happy about this," she mumbled as she turned to face him. Sunlight glinted in her dark hair and highlighted her high cheekbones. Her eyes flashed with frustration, but her hand was gentle as she patted Sophia's back.

She hadn't asked for the trouble she was in.

He had to keep that in mind when he dealt with her. She wasn't a hardened criminal, a drug addict, a con man. She was a young woman who'd done everything right.

Except when it came to choosing her husband.

"I know," he said calmly. "I'm not thrilled, either, but this isn't about how either of us feels."

"No. It's not. It's about getting me to trial and getting the men who killed my husband convicted." She brushed a piece of hair off her cheek, her hand shaking.

It was the truth, a kind of truth Hunter dealt with every day. His job wasn't ever about the lives he was protecting; it was always about justice.

Usually, that didn't bother him.

Right then, looking at Annie and Sophia, he felt almost guilty about it.

"It's about more than that, Annie. I made a promise to you when this started. I told you that I'd protect you while you waited for trial. I always keep my word."

"Unless the person you gave your word to jumps out of a moving vehicle?" she said with a slight smile.

"Even then, I keep my word," he said, taking her arm and moving her away from the doors. She was nearly a foot shorter than him, her head barely reaching his shoulders. Not delicate, but not the kind of tall, athletic woman he usually hung around with.

She wasn't needy, though.

As a matter of fact, her independent streak was starting to get in the way of his job. He wasn't happy about that, but lecturing her on the foolishness of what she'd done wouldn't change it. All he could do was hope and pray that she didn't repeat the mistake. Not that he was much for either hoping or praying.

He tended to trust himself and his instincts rather than waiting around for God to give him help and portents. He was willing to admit it, but not all that proud of the fact. His mother had brought him to church every Sunday for as long as he could remember. His father had attended on holidays if he hadn't been working. More often than not, he had been. Always too busy for everyone. Including God. That had been his father's M.O.

Now it seemed to be Hunter's. If not for the fact that Annie insisted on attending church every Sunday, he would probably have spent every Sunday morning for the past month in bed or at the gym.

He hadn't ever felt guilty about that, but lately, he'd begun to crave the peace of Sunday-morning worship, the fellowship that came from spending time with people who had the same values and beliefs as he did. It was a new feeling, and not an unwelcome one. Church and faith had been a mainstay of his childhood. He was more than happy to have it be a mainstay again.

He led Annie back through the lobby, walking her out into a parking lot behind the building. He'd had Serena transfer Sophia's car seat into his SUV, and he opened the door quickly, ushering Annie into the backseat. He let her clip Sophia in while he called Burke. He'd sent the rest of the team ahead to secure the house. They were the only ones who knew that the meeting was over and that Annie was on the move again.

If something happened in transit, Hunter would know that the betrayer was someone on the team. He'd planned it that way, was prepared for trouble, but he couldn't believe it would come, didn't want to believe that any of the people he trusted wasn't trustworthy.

"Ready?" he asked, glancing into the rearview mirror.

"What about the meeting with Steve?"

"Postponed."

"Then I guess we've got nothing better to do," Annie responded. "Home, James!"

He almost laughed at that. Almost. But he was working, and he couldn't afford to be distracted by Annie.

He pulled out of the parking lot, glancing in the rearview mirror. Just to be sure he wasn't being followed.

Nothing moved. No shadows, no hints that someone was waiting for the opportunity to fall into place behind him. He wound his way through downtown St. Louis, followed traffic onto the freeway, exited and backtracked. Still nothing.

Sophia started singing a Christmas song. The words were two-year-old gibberish, but the tune sounded an awful lot like "Silent Night." Not bad for a little kid. By the next Christmas, she'd be singing the words clearly. A year after that, she'd probably be standing up in front of church making half the congregation cry with her sweet, pure voice.

He frowned, not quite sure why he was thinking about the next year and the one after that. By that time, Sophia and Annie would be settled into their new lives. They'd be far away from St. Louis. Hunter would have no reason to know what they were doing, where they were attending church, how well they were getting on in their new lives. Saying goodbye to clients had never bothered him before. This time, the idea of it ate away at him.

Annie had her head back and her eyes closed, her soft dark hair brushing her shoulders. She looked relaxed and gorgeous, and he couldn't help wondering what it would have been like to meet her years ago. When he'd been just starting out in his career and she'd just started college. Before his commitment to the marshals and her marriage to Joe. She wasn't his type, but he thought that they would have connected, that he would have seen in her all the things that were missing in him. Maybe he might have given himself over to that. For a while.

And then he would have broken her heart and his own.

It was an odd thing to be thinking about. Not something he was comfortable with, but not something he was going to ignore, either. He might have a lot of faults, but lying to himself wasn't one of them. The more time he spent with Annie, the more time he wanted to spend with her. That was a fact, and it wasn't one that he could change by ignoring it.

That didn't mean he had to act on it.

She was a witness. He was her protector.

It was as simple as that.

All he had to do was keep from complicating it.

He exited the freeway again, traveled through a residential area and into a newish community with large single-family homes and oversize town houses. He'd lived in a town house there for a couple of years, but he'd gotten tired of sharing walls with his neighbors. He probably would have stayed there anyway, but Burke had been looking for a bachelor pad, a larger place than the apartment he was in. He hadn't wanted to shoulder the cost of home ownership alone, so he asked if Hunter wanted to rent with him. Hunter had been in just the right frame of mind to say yes.

He hadn't regretted it.

But then, he rarely regretted his decisions. He spent too much time thinking them through, planning for every inevitability, weighing the pros and cons.

A dark car pulled in behind him, speeding out of a driveway and hugging his bumper. He tensed, his hands tightening on the steering wheel.

Annie shifted in her seat and glanced out the back window. "What's going on?"

He turned onto a side street, frowning as the car turned with him. "Just being cautious."

"Because of the car behind us?"

"Because I'm worried about anything and everything that might pose a threat to you and your daughter." He accelerated, speeding through the community and back onto the highway, calling in their location and asking for backup as he zipped along the interstate.

The car stayed close, keeping pace with Hunter.

Not threatening in any way, but Hunter never took chances, never underestimated the desperation of the enemy.

"What if—?" Annie started to ask.

"Everything is going to be fine." He cut her off because his attention had to be on the road and on the car that seemed to be following them.

Would it be fine?

Annie didn't think so. Not if the person in the car behind them opened fire with a gun or side-swiped Hunter's car. "How can it be fine if we're being tailed?"

"I don't know that we are."

"Then—"

"I'm being cautious, Annie. It's the only way to keep you and Sophia safe."

He passed a semitruck, glanced in the rearview mirror, no emotion on his face. If he were worried, she couldn't tell. But that was Hunter's way. She couldn't take any comfort in it.

Her heart thudded painfully, and she felt sick, her stomach churning. She wanted to be back in Milwaukee, living the new life that she'd carved for herself. Better yet, she wanted to go back in time, get to the house she and Joe had shared before he was murdered.

The sound of sirens drifted into the car, and she turned to look out the back window. A police cruiser pulled behind the car that was following them. Seconds later, both vehicles pulled over.

Hunter kept driving.

"Are you going back to see what's going on?" she asked.

"If the driver of that car is anyone to worry about, the police will let me know."

"And then what?"

"We'll have to move you again. For now, though, we're going to stick to the plan."

Of course they were.

Hunter always followed the plan.

She frowned, craning her neck to see what was going on behind them. They'd already pulled so far ahead that she couldn't see anything more than police cars.

"Don't you ever break the rules, Hunter?" she asked.

"Not when it comes to my job. Lives depend on me doing what I'm supposed to do, the way I'm supposed to do it."

She couldn't complain about that, couldn't resent it. Because of him, she and Sophia had been safe for a year. She let the subject drop, tried to focus on something other than the car that might or might not have been following them.

"How much longer do you think we'll be driving around? I think Sophia is about to fall asleep, and if she does, I'll be up half the night with her."

"Not long."

"Way to be specific," she muttered.

"I always aim to please," he replied, surprising a laugh out of her.

"I didn't know you had a sense of humor, Hunter."

"There's a lot you don't know about me." He smiled as he exited the freeway.

"Like?"

"I've enjoyed going to church with you on Sunday mornings. I hadn't been in a while, and it's been nice to get back into the routine of Sunday worship."

"Really? I thought you probably hated it."

"You were wrong." His cell phone rang, and he answered, listening intently for a moment. "Okay. Good to know. Thanks for checking things out."

He hung up. "We're in good shape," he said. "The guy in the car was on his way to work. Didn't even know we existed."

"He must have been scared out of his mind when the police pulled him over like that."

"He was going twenty miles an hour above the speed limit, so there was good reason to pull him over. Besides, it's better to have him scared than have you dead."

"Cookies!" Sophia yelled, breaking into their conversation.

"You have to wait, Sophia," Annie responded.

"I think I have some crackers in my bag. It's on the floor," Hunter offered.

"Cookies!" Sophia replied.

"Crackers," Annie responded.

"No. Cookies."

"Yep. You're ready for bed," Annie muttered as she found Hunter's backpack and opened it. She handed Sophia a cracker as Hunter drove through a neighborhood of 1920s homes.

"Want a cracker?" Annie asked, leaning over the seat, her hand brushing Hunter's shoulder. Her stomach twisted in response, warmth shooting through her blood.

"No. Thanks."

Hunter didn't want a cracker. He also didn't want Annie's arm brushing against his, her breath fanning the side of his neck as she leaned over the seat. He took the package from her hand, anything to get her back in her seat and away from him.

"I might have one later," he muttered, dropping the crackers onto the seat beside him.

He'd been working too hard. That was the problem. He'd worked Christmas this year. New Year's Eve. New Year's Day. He'd worked every weekend since Annie had come back to town. If he wasn't guarding her, he was at the office, digging through old and new leads in Daniel's murder investigation.

Last year had been tough.

This year had to be better.

The house was up ahead. Burke's car was parked to the side, the garage door open. He pulled in, hit the button to close the door.

"Yay! We're here!" Annie said cheerfully.

"Yay!" Sophia clapped her hands.

They might not be as excited when they got inside. Josh and Serena had been given the task of preparing a room. The way those two had been getting along, Hunter would be surprised if they'd managed to do anything more than argue.

Annie climbed out of the SUV before he got around to her door. She was leaning in, unbuckling Sophia by the time he reached her side. Her denim jeans clung to long lean legs, her dark hair falling just past her shoulders. It always seemed shiny and bouncy. No hair spray or hair gels. Nothing but clean.

He liked that about her.

She was no frills. No demands for makeup or hair supplies. Unlike her husband, she didn't seem to be striving for more than what she needed. Joe had made a big mistake in that. Interviews with people who'd known him had revealed a man who didn't know what contentment meant. Even after he'd married his high school and college sweetheart, even after they'd had a daughter, he'd always been looking for more.

That was what his gambling buddies had said.

It was what his friends and coworkers had said.

Only Annie hadn't said that.

Whatever her opinion of her husband, she kept it to herself. Anything she did say was complimentary. Maybe for Sophia's sake, or maybe just because she was too loyal to speak poorly of the dead.

She turned with Sophia in her arms, nearly bumping into him.

"Sorry." Her cheeks were pink, her gaze lowered, her battered bandaged knees peeking out from ripped and shredded jeans. She'd jumped from a moving vehicle to get to her daughter.

She was Hunter's job.

She was also a woman, a mother, a daughter and friend. A widow who'd been through too much.

There was always humanity in the midst of his work. He just chose to focus on other things.

Lately, he was finding that a lot more difficult than he wanted it to be.

"The door is this way." He took her arm, his fingers sliding around firm muscles and soft fabric. A small laundry room separated the garage from the main house.

Hunter and Burke didn't spend a ton of time at home. Sometimes, Burke had a date over for dinner. Usually, though, the kitchen stayed empty. The large backyard stayed empty. The communal living areas stayed empty. Because of that, the house would be the perfect place to hide Annie and Sophia for a few weeks.

They walked through the laundry room and into the kitchen.

A computer sat on the round kitchen table, the monitor set to display images from the security cameras that he and Burke had installed after they moved in.

Always better to be safe than sorry, and in their job, enemies were always an issue.

Someone had started a pot of coffee. Hunter didn't think he needed any more caffeine, but he grabbed a mug from the cupboard anyway and poured some into it.

"Coffee?" he asked Annie.

"No. Thanks." She glanced around the large room. "Where is everyone?"

"Probably upstairs getting your room ready." He opened the fridge. There wasn't a whole lot to choose from. He and Burke hadn't been expecting company. "Are you hungry, Sophia?"

The little girl shook her head, her eyes half-closed, her cheek resting against Annie's shoulder. She had her thumb in her mouth and her free hand woven through the ends of Annie's hair.

"You need to eat anyway, sweetie." Annie patted her daughter's back. "Are there eggs? Maybe I can scramble some for her."

"A dozen." He pulled the carton off the shelf, grabbed a pan from the drawer under the oven and a bowl from a cupboard.

"I don't think she'll eat that many, but thanks." She smiled as she set Sophia down.

"There's sausage, too, if she'll eat it."

"I think the eggs will be enough. And maybe some toast."

"Sure." He pulled a loaf of bread from an old-fashioned bread box that Burke had inherited from his grandmother.

The floor above his head creaked. Something slid across the wood. Good. They were actually getting something done.

He glanced at the computer monitors. The street was quiet, dusk falling in deep shades of purple and gray. Someone had already closed the window shades in the kitchen. He glanced into the living room. Same there.

"Do you think you can stay inside while I go upstairs and check on the progress?" he asked. He didn't bother telling her that there were alarms on all the doors and windows. It would be interesting to see if she tried to run again.

"Where else would I go?" she asked as she cracked an egg into the bowl.

"The same place you were planning to go when you jumped out of the car."

"I was going to Sophia. Since she's with me, I think I'll just stay put for a while."

A while didn't mean until the trial.

Hunter was pretty certain that she had purposely worded her response that way.

He kept his mouth shut about it, though, and walked through the kitchen and up the stairs.

NINE

Obviously, there were alarms on the doors and the windows.

There was absolutely no way Hunter would have left her and Sophia alone otherwise.

Annie whisked two eggs in the bowl and searched through the cupboards for salt and pepper, Sophia clinging to her leg the whole time.

She hadn't had a nap and her schedule was off. Annie couldn't blame her for whining and clinging.

On the other hand, Annie hadn't slept well. She wanted to whine and cling, too. The problem was, she didn't have anyone to complain to and she didn't have anyone to cling to, either. That had been the best thing about marriage. Always having someone there. Always knowing that she wasn't on her own and that, if she was having a bad day, she had someone to pick up the slack.

Most of the time, she didn't let the lack of those things bother her. She just went about her days doing what she needed to. Every once in a while, she wished she could have the life she'd planned. The one she and Joe had dreamed of.

Even if he'd lived, they wouldn't have had it, though. With the amount of debt Joe had accrued during their short marriage, they'd have lost their home eventually. They'd have lost their car. They probably would have fought even more than they already had been about finances.

The happy life they'd been planning would have been buried under the burden of Joe's addiction.

She poured the eggs into the pan and cooked them quickly, her throat tight with everything she'd lost.

She dropped toast into the toaster, the sound of something being dragged across the floor above her head scraping along her nerves. She felt trapped, and she didn't like the feeling.

She didn't know what to do about it, either.

Except pray. She'd done so much of *that* in the past year, she was sure God must be tired of hearing the same requests over and over again.

Please, keep Sophia safe.

Please, get me through the trial.

Please, let us just get a normal life back.

She wanted all those things so badly. She knew she had to trust that God would provide them. Trust was hard lately, though. *Everything* was hard.

She slid the eggs onto a plate, buttered a piece of toast and looked around the kitchen. There wasn't a place for Sophia to eat unless she had her sit at the table right near the computer. A toddler, eggs and a computer didn't seem like a good mix, so she carried everything out of the kitchen and into a large living room. The furniture looked new, the hardwood floor polished to a high shine. Beyond the room, a staircase led up to a second floor. Just beyond that, another room opened up. It didn't look like a dining room. At least, it didn't seem to have a table or chairs in it.

The living room would have to work. Nothing in it looked baby-proof, but she carried the plate to the coffee table and set it there.

"Here, Sophia," she said. "Let's eat."

She forked up some eggs.

"No!" Sophia said, swiping at the fork. "I do it."

Egg splattered on the floor and slid halfway across the room.

Wonderful!

Annie hurried into the kitchen, grabbed a dish towel from the sink and ran back into the living room. It took about twenty seconds, but by the time she got back, more eggs were on the floor and somehow Sophia had smashed a handful of them into her hair.

Leaving the plate on the table had been a rookie mistake. She knew better. She'd just been too tired to think things through.

"Sophia!" she nearly yelled as her daughter grabbed another handful of eggs. "Don't!"

Too late…

Eggs flew across the room, landed on the edge of the black leather sofa and slid to the floor.

Annie grabbed the plate. She was about ready to tear her hair out, but that wouldn't do anyone any good.

Hot tears burned behind her eyes. To her horror, one slipped down her cheek.

"There's no sense crying over tossed eggs," she muttered as she wiped egg off the floor. Another tear slipped down her face.

It seemed so ridiculous to be crying because her daughter had chucked egg all over the room, but she was.

She sniffed back more tears and wiped down the sofa. Thankfully, it didn't look as though the leather had been damaged. A few more spots of egg, and the room would be clean. Then she'd just have to give Sophia a bath, scrub her hair and dry it so that she didn't have to go to bed with it wet.

She knelt on the floor, wiping slimy egg from the wood, her bandaged knees throbbing. The entire day had been a mess. Compared to everything else, the eggs shouldn't have been a big deal.

So, why did they feel like they were?

Sophia headed for the stairs, and Annie scooped her up one-armed. "No, Sophia! Sit down and be good while Mommy finishes cleaning up your mess," she snapped.

Sophia giggled.

She was in the mood for games.

Annie was not.

She carried Sophia into the kitchen, rinsed out the dishrag, her palms stinging. She grabbed a piece of paper towel, wet it in the sink and started washing Sophia's face and hands. Apparently, her daughter did not want to be cleaned. She squealed and wiggled, her protests escalating to a full-blown shriek that settled right into the space behind Annie's eyes.

"Everything okay in here?" Hunter asked as he walked into the kitchen. A plate of food sat on the counter, a piece of toast and a few smashed bits of egg sitting on it.

Annie was at the sink, Sophia screaming as she tried to wash her face. Somehow, the kid had gotten egg in her hair. And on her shirt. And, actually, now that he was looking, on the floor.

"We're fine," Annie muttered, wiping Sophia's face one more time before she set her on the floor. Neither looked fine. Sophia looked fit to be tied, and Annie looked as if she'd been crying, her eyes red-rimmed and glittering with more tears.

"It looks like someone needs a bath," he said calmly. Defusing an escalating situation was part of the job description. Even if the escalating situation was an overtired toddler. "You ready for a bath, Sophia?"

"No!" she shrieked, stomping her foot for emphasis.

Annie sighed. "I guess this is it. The beginning of the terrible twos." Her voice wobbled a little, but she didn't shed the tears that were in her eyes.

"My sister says the twos are easy. It's the threes you have to watch out for." He opened a cupboard, looking for something that might fill Sophia's mouth and keep her from crying.

"Thanks for the words of encouragement," Annie said drily. "And if you're hunting for a treat for my defiant little girl, forget it. She's taking a bath, and then she's going to bed."

"She's just overtired."

"I know that, but…" She pressed her lips together and lifted her daughter.

"What?"

"I'm overtired, too, and being in protective custody is starting to get to me."

"What do you need to make things better?" he asked, telling himself that he had to keep her happy, keep her focused and heading happily toward trial.

There were other reasons he wanted to know, reasons that had more to do with who Annie was than what she could do for the prosecuting attorney's case.

"Nothing that you can give me right now."

"Tell me anyway."

"Why?" she asked, lifting Sophia and carrying her from the room. She was limping slightly. Probably from the long gash on her knee.

"Because it's—"

"Your job to make sure that I'm comfortable, happy and safe?" She glanced over her shoulder, her blue eyes hard. "I think we've been over this a thousand times in the past couple of months, and I don't need the reminder. How about you just show me where the bathroom is so I can wash Sophia's hair? Hopefully, by the time I'm done, her bed will be ready."

He grabbed her arm before she could walk away, holding her in place.

"I was going to say," he murmured, "that it's possible to get around some of our safeguards. Or maybe a better way to say it would be that we can work within those safeguards and still give you a little more freedom, if that's what you need."

"Oh." Her cheeks blazed, but she looked straight into his eyes. "Sorry. I guess this is my day for jumping to conclusions."

"It's been a long month."

"It's been a long year."

And it had obviously taken its toll on her. She was at least ten pounds lighter than when they'd met, her eyes deeply shadowed. Her normal good cheer usually hid that, but today, he could see the fatigue on her face.

"It will be over soon, Annie. The trial is just around the corner," he assured her, sliding his hand from her arm to her shoulder, letting his palm rest there.

"It's never going to be over. Everything I wanted is out of my reach, and I'm going to have to spend the rest of my life dealing with that."

"What did you want?"

"Just…family. A nice little house where I could be happy."

"You can still have those things," he reminded her.

"Maybe so, but it won't ever be the same. I'll always have Joe's…" She glanced at her daughter and pressed her lips together. "The past will always be part of my life. I can't change it, and I can't pretend it didn't happen."

"But you can move on, make something even better than what you had."

"Maybe," she said with a sad smile that made his heart ache. "I really need to get Sophia into the bath. Can you show me where it is now?"

He wanted to tell her that she had deserved better than a husband who sneaked around behind her back, spending money neither of them had. He wanted to tell her that, in a few years, she really would have everything she'd lost. Maybe even more.

He wanted to tell her that she shouldn't let the past limit the future, but it wasn't his right, so he stayed silent.

He led her up the stairs instead, showed her the oversize bathroom. A claw-foot tub sat beneath a window, an old-fashioned showerhead hanging above it.

He pulled towels from the linen closet and found a small bottle of baby shampoo that his sister had left after she'd visited with her kids.

He set them on the edge of the sink.

"Serena and Josh stopped by the safe house on the way here and grabbed your suitcase. I—"

"Really?" Annie asked. "That's great. Can I get a few things out of it?"

"Sure. Your room is down the hall." He led her to the room that he and Burke used for guests. Not that they had many. Burke's sister came once in a blue moon, and Hunter's sister and nephews stayed the night when they were in town. Once or twice a year at most.

Josh was pushing the newly built crib into place as Hunter entered the room. Burke had dismantled it the previous day, planning to move it to the apartment.

"I think we're finished," Josh said. "Mind if I head out? I have some paperwork to do at the office before my shift ends."

Hunter was tempted to ask what Josh's hurry was,

but he thought he knew. There was enough tension in the air to choke a man, and most of it was coming from Serena.

"No problem," he responded. "Where's the suitcase you brought from the safe house?"

"I put it in the closet when we were moving furniture around," Josh said. "I'll get it."

"Don't worry about it, Josh. I can handle it. You go do your paperwork," Serena cut in, her voice smooth and cool. She'd always been a consummate professional, but since her brother's death, she seemed to have an impenetrable veneer. Always professional. Always calm. Always coolly in control.

Josh nodded and left the room, his shoulders tense, his carriage upright. He looked angry and a little hurt.

Not surprising. He'd lost a lot when Daniel died. Not just his partner, but his best friend. Hunter almost went after him. Just to make sure he was doing okay, but he didn't think Josh would appreciate that he'd noticed his weakness or, even, that he was worried for him.

"Here's the suitcase," Serena said, dropping it onto the bed. "I thought I'd make a run to the store, grab a few more things that we're probably going to need. Juice. Cereal. Baby stuff."

"Sounds good."

"Is there anything you want or need, Annie?" she asked.

Annie was already unzipping the suitcase, Sophia still fussing in her arms. She shook her head. "No, thanks."

"Have Hunter call me if you change your mind." Serena walked into the hall and turned to face Hunter again. "When will Burke be back?"

"A couple of hours. He's meeting with the computer forensic team."

"Shouldn't you be there? I can stay here if you want to attend the meeting."

"Burke can handle it." And Hunter didn't really trust Annie to stay put.

She might, for her daughter's sake, but he sensed her restlessness and her fear. Even if she hadn't admitted that she was tired of being in witness protection, he would have known it.

"Sounds good. I'll see you in a couple of hours. If there's any trouble, you know where to find me."

"There won't be."

He hoped.

Serena hurried down the hall, her feet pounding on the wood stairs. He heard the door open and close, heard the dead bolt turn. She'd set the alarm. That was part of protocol, and he trusted her to follow it.

Outside, the wind had picked up, battering the windows and whistling through the eaves. If Annie noticed, she didn't let on. Just kept pulling things out of the suitcase. Pink pajamas. A soft white blanket.

A little brown dog. She unzipped a side pocket and pulled out a bottle of baby wash and a small washcloth. Like every mother he'd ever known, she was prepared.

She pulled a black Bible from the front pocket and set it on the bed. He'd seen that Bible a hundred times, but something about the way she touched the front cover made him wonder where it had come from, how long she'd had it, who had given it to her.

"I think that's all I need." She left the suitcase unzipped and walked out into the hall. "Thank you, Hunter."

He'd been dismissed.

He heard the bathroom door close. Water splashed into the tub. The sounds of everyday life for a widow and her daughter.

He should have walked out of the room right then. Gone downstairs and waited for the others to return. He lifted the Bible instead. The leather was soft with use, the pages thin, their edges bent and curled. It didn't feel intrusive to open it. Maybe because he'd spent nearly a decade standing on the outside of other people's lives, studying their habits, learning their routines. Keeping them safe always meant knowing everything about them. He became part of their lives while staying completely separate from them. That was how he lived with the witnesses he was protecting.

He opened the faded cover of the Bible to a presentation page.

To my first and only love. May we have forever and a day together. Love, Joe.

The inscription was dated. It could have been presented on any day, but Hunter knew the date. He'd studied Annie's life. Learned who her friends were, what her past was, where all her connections lay. He'd needed to make sure that she didn't return to any old habits or old friends, that she didn't find herself tempted to connect to anyone she'd known before her husband's murder.

Yeah. He knew the date. Knew it was the day she'd married Joe Delacorte. His wedding gift to her? Probably.

Suddenly, he *did* feel as though he was intruding. As if he was glimpsing something too personal, something that was absolutely none of his business.

Why she'd kept a Bible given to her by a man who'd lied to her, betrayed her trust, gotten her into the kind of trouble most people would never see in a lifetime, wasn't anything he needed to know.

He set the Bible down and walked out of the room, past the bathroom, where he could hear Annie singing some silly kid song to her daughter, down the stairs, where the house looked just like it had before Annie and her daughter had arrived.

It felt different, though.

It felt a lot more like home.

TEN

Sophia fell asleep quickly, her cheeks pink from her warm bath, her thumb in her mouth. Tendrils of hair curled at her nape and stuck to her forehead, while her long lashes brushed her cheeks.

Sleeping, she looked like Joe, full-cheeked and round-faced. Her coloring was more Annie's, but the resemblance to her father was there in the cheeks and lashes and full lips.

The windowpane rattled, a winter storm blowing outside.

The rule was, stay away from the windows. Hunter had told her that fifty times since she'd walked into his house.

She was tempted to go peek outside anyway.

She'd always loved storms. The howling wind and blowing rain or snow. The wild whipping of trees and bushes.

Aside from the rattling windows, the house was silent. Burke had returned with take-out Chinese for dinner. They'd all eaten in the kitchen, the conversation stilted and strained. It felt...weird being in a house that was lived in rather than one that was just used to keep witnesses safe.

It felt even stranger to know that it was Hunter's house.

That he'd actually brought her there seemed outside his character, but maybe she didn't really know what his character was.

By the book, but there were other parts of him.

Things she was just starting to notice, and that she wished she weren't. Like how gentle he'd been when he was bandaging her knees.

She paced across the room, her palm itching to pull back the curtain, open the shades and stare out into the wild night.

She'd felt restless all day, frustrated and discontent. That wasn't like her. If she could sleep, maybe she could get over her mood, but she was wide-awake at...

She glanced at the clock on the nightstand. One in the morning. Maybe a cup of warm milk would help her sleep, but she hated milk.

So, maybe a cup of green tea.

Did men like Burke and Hunter drink green tea? There was no time like the present to find out.

She crept to the door and eased it open.

The hallway was dark, no lights showing from the rooms below. The stairs creaked. She knew that either Burke or Hunter was probably awake, probably listening to the creaking stairs and probably wondering what she was doing.

She made it to the bottom of the stairs and was halfway across the living room when the light went on.

"What's up?" Hunter asked, his broad frame blocking the kitchen doorway. He'd changed into faded jeans and a light blue T-shirt, his gun holster strapped to his chest. He looked more like a bodyguard than he ever had and more like a man than she wanted to notice.

"I couldn't sleep," she admitted.

"Too much on your mind?"

"I guess."

"That's not surprising. It's been a long day." He crossed the room and cupped her elbow. "How about some green tea?"

"That's exactly what I was coming to look for," she responded. "You must have been reading my mind."

"Just watching you for the past few weeks."

"I'm not even sure what to say to that."

"It's just part of my job, Annie. Nothing for you to feel uncomfortable about."

"Who says I'm uncomfortable?"

"Your cheeks are pink and your nostrils are flaring."

"No, they're not," she said, her hand flying up to cover her nose.

He chuckled and pulled her into the kitchen. "I was kidding about your nostrils, but your cheeks are pink."

"You kid?" she asked as she grabbed an old-fashioned teakettle from the stove.

"Only with people I like."

"You like people?"

He laughed at that, the sound filling the kitchen and weaving threads around her heart. She felt them tugging her toward him.

Maybe tea wasn't such a good idea, but going back to the room seemed like an even worse one. More time alone. More time to think and pace and worry and remember.

"I do like people," he said as he reached above her head and pulled out a box of tea. His chest brushed her back, the scent of soap and masculinity surrounding her.

"Especially people who are law-abiding citizens," he murmured in her ear, and she knew her cheeks were pink again. Maybe fire-engine red.

"Who says I'm law-abiding?" She ducked away, her heart thumping painfully.

"Your file." He took a package of vanilla sandwich cookies from the cupboard. They hadn't been there earlier. Obviously, Burke had brought them back with the Chinese food. Her guilty pleasure. Even Joe had never known how addicted to the silly things she was.

"I have a file?"

"Sure."

"I'm not sure I like that." She didn't reach for the cookies, but she was tempted.

"It's nothing to like or not like. It's just what we do."

"*We* meaning the corporate organization that is the U.S. Marshals?"

"Something like that." He opened the cookies and ate one.

"What's in my file?" She really wanted to know. "Information about my childhood? Do you know that I was suspended from school when I was in fourth grade?"

"You were suspended?" He eyed her as if he were sure she was lying. "For what?"

"Protesting. I thought it was unfair that the fifth graders got to go on an overnight field trip and the fourth graders didn't. I made a sign and picketed the school."

"No way."

"It's true. I marched in front of the school door until the principal called my mother. She pulled up in her old Cadillac Seville, and I decided maybe I didn't need to protest anymore."

"I wish I could have seen that, Annie." He chuckled as he grabbed a mug from the cupboard and handed it to her.

"It wasn't nearly as impressive as it sounds. I'd

tried to get my friends to participate, but they all chickened out, so I was standing out there alone with my sign." She poured hot water into the cup and dunked a bag in it.

"A rebel without a cause?"

"A general without an army." She sat down at the table, still ignoring the cookies. "It all worked out, though. I ended up meeting Joe because of it."

"Yeah?" Hunter glanced at the computer monitor, then poured himself a glass of orange juice. He didn't ask about Joe, and she could have just kept her mouth shut, kept the story to herself, because it wasn't something she really wanted to talk about.

After all, Joe had been the best and the worst thing that had ever happened to her.

But the words poured out anyway. "My rebellion wasn't that impressive, but my reputation for it preceded me to middle school. I got elected president of the student body without even running. Joe was vice president. He loved politics and debate. Did you know he studied political science in college?"

"Yes," he said quietly, his gaze unwavering. He knew how to listen, his body leaning toward her, every bit of his attention focused on the conversation.

"He had these great plans and dreams. He was going to run for city council and eventually run for the state legislature, but then we got married, and he put those dreams aside so he could support the family. That's why he was driving trucks for a living."

"You're giving him too much credit, Annie, and I think you know it."

"You mean because he was using all his trips to gamble away our life savings?" She sipped her tea, her eyes hot and gritty with unshed tears. "I know what he did, but I don't think he planned things to happen the way they turned out. I think he really thought he was doing what was best for our family."

"That's because you're a good person, and you like to see the good in the people around you." He brushed a piece of hair from her cheek and tucked it behind her ear, his fingers lingering for a moment.

The tender gesture surprised her, and she leaned back.

"I'm not that good, Hunter. I'm angry just like any other person in my situation would be," she said, refusing to acknowledge the butterflies that were dancing in her stomach…

This was Hunter. Not some handsome man that she'd met at church or the grocery store or, even, some online dating site.

"You never act angry. I haven't heard you say one bad word against your husband," he pointed out.

"What good would it do? He's gone. He can't repent or ask forgiveness. He can't change what he did or try to make things better."

"There are plenty of people who wouldn't care

about that. They'd spend the rest of their lives complaining about the wrongs that were done to them."

He was right. Her parents had said an earful when she'd told them about Joe's debt, about his gambling and his lies. They'd probably still be saying those things to her if she hadn't been in witness protection. She'd have to be careful. When the time came, and she was able to contact her parents again, they'd have to watch what they said around Sophia.

"I'm not one of them."

"I've noticed." He settled into a chair, his legs stretched out and crossed at the ankles. He had long legs, muscular thighs and an easy way of moving that said he was comfortable in his own skin.

She was usually the same way.

Right then, she didn't feel comfortable.

She felt…aware.

Of Hunter. Of herself. Of the space that separated them and of how easy it would be to cross it.

She fiddled with a dishcloth, wiping down the counter even though it was spotless. "You notice a lot. I'm not sure I like it."

"It's just part of the job, Annie. Nothing to be upset about."

"You keep saying that."

"Because it keeps being true."

"Well, maybe it would be an easier truth for me to swallow if you weren't the one making all the decisions and calling all the shots."

"Is that why you jumped out of the car this morning? Because you were tired of letting me take control?"

"I jumped out of the car because you lied to me, and I realized I had to take care of things myself," she answered truthfully. There was no sense in trying to deny it.

He frowned. "Lied about what?"

"You said that Josh and Serena were taking Sophia to headquarters. I looked out the car window and saw her in the crowd."

"Where did you think she was going to be?"

"In a car, heading away from the fire. Just like we were."

"She was on her way to the car. They were up in the apartment when the bomb exploded, remember? They had to take the stairs down with everyone else who lives in the apartment. Serena ran down ahead, got her car and drove around to pick Josh and Sophia up. If you'd done what I told you and stayed in the car, there wouldn't have been any hitch in their plan or its execution."

"If you had a daughter, you would have done exactly what I did."

He didn't deny it, just took another cookie and ate it.

Her stomach growled, but she wasn't in the mood for eating. Not even her favorite cookies.

"Here's the deal," Hunter finally said. "You're a

great mother. A really great one. I understand why you felt like you had to get to your daughter, but it is my job to keep you both safe. No matter the circumstances, no matter how worried you are, you've got to trust me to do that."

"Why?" she asked. "Because you're a U.S. marshal? That's not enough for me."

"Because I care about you and Sophia, and because I would never lie to you."

"I've heard that before," she snorted, turning away because she didn't want him to see the pain in her eyes and on her face.

"From Joe?" Hunter asked. "I don't think his word counted for much."

"It did to me. It counted for everything."

"He didn't deserve your trust, Annie. He didn't deserve the faith you put in him."

"But you do?" She swung around, her heart fluttering when she realized that he'd crossed the room, was standing so close she could smell soap and shampoo and feel the heat of his body through her jeans and T-shirt.

"I'd like to think that I do," he responded easily, his eyes so dark they were almost black. "I'd like to think that I've proved it to you over and over again in the past year. I'd like to think that every time I called you in Milwaukee to see how you were doing and ask if you needed anything, every time I went out of my way to make sure you and Sophia had what you needed, every time I took you to church on Sunday morning, I proved that I wanted what was best for you and your daughter."

He had. She couldn't deny that any more than she could stop the wild throb of her heart when she looked into his eyes. "I think I should go to bed. It's late, and Sophia will be up early."

She sidled past him, would have left the kitchen, but he snagged the back of her shirt. "Running away, Annie?"

"Going to bed, Hunter."

He laughed and released his hold. "Going to pace your room and wait until the sun comes up is more like it."

He'd hit the nail on the head, but she didn't plan to admit it. "You should probably go to sleep, too. We've both had a long day."

"I'm working my shift. I don't think I can do that very well while I'm sleeping."

"You worked this morning."

"Until we know how you're being found, only four of us will know you're here. Burke, Josh, Serena and I will be working overtime the next two weeks."

So, they were putting their lives on hold until the trial. She'd put her life on hold for a year, and she knew just how it felt to give up time with friends and family for the sake of someone or something else.

"I'm sorry, Hunter," she said.

"For what?"

"Causing so much trouble for all of you."

"You haven't caused anything. As a matter of fact, you've been easier to protect than any witness I've ever worked with." His lips quirked in a half smile. "If we don't count today."

"Can we not?"

"If you promise not to go maverick on me again. I want you safe, Annie. I want to get you through the trial and back to the life you deserve."

"What life is that? I don't think I even know anymore."

"A life where you can go to work and church without worrying about having a bodyguard tagging along behind. A life where you can take your daughter to the playground." He took her hand and pulled her a step closer. "A life where you can be Annie or Angel or whoever you want to be."

For some reason, his words made her throat tight and her chest heavy. "Do you think that's really going to happen? Because, right now, it seems like my life is always going to be just like it is right now."

"You've been through a lot this year, but it *will* end. I promise you that."

"I don't need promises. I just need…"

"What?" He looked as if he really cared, his attention completely focused on her, his hand warm and calloused and, somehow, absolutely wonderful.

"To go back in time and start over again."

That was a truth she hadn't even admitted to herself.

Not until that moment.

"With your marriage?"

"Yes. No." She sighed. "I don't know. I'd like to think that I'd do things differently, but who's to say?"

"It would be nice if life had a redo button. That's for sure," he agreed, tugging her back across the room and urging her into a chair. "Tell you what. How about you drink your tea, have a cookie and tell me what you'd do differently if God gave you a do-over."

He set her teacup on the table and took the seat next to her. Their legs were touching, their arms pressed closer than Annie should have wanted.

She didn't move, though. Didn't back away or try to put some distance between them because sitting there with Hunter felt so much better than anything had in a long time, and she really wasn't sure she wanted it to end.

ELEVEN

Hunter shoved the package of cookies toward Annie and watched while she took two. Her cheeks were flushed pink, her hair spilled over her shoulders. She'd changed into faded jeans and a fitted T-shirt, a well-worn cardigan over it. The sweater didn't look like something Annie would choose. Dark blue with thick black horizontal stripes, it looked more like a man's sweater than a woman's.

Joe's?

Probably, and he wasn't sure why that bothered him, or why he wanted to drag the sweater off her shoulders and toss it into the fireplace with a starter log and a few matches.

Or maybe he did know. Maybe he just didn't want to admit it.

"I love these things," Annie murmured as she bit into one of the cookies.

"I've noticed."

"What does that mean?" She watched him suspiciously.

"You asked me to get you some your first day back in town."

"I did?" She looked at the cookie and frowned.

"Yes. The day after that, you asked for more. I think I've bought six packages of those the past month."

She shrugged. "As vices go, it's not a bad one."

"I could help you find a different one."

"Like?"

"Target practice. Long walks. Hikes through the woods."

"Are those your favorite activities?"

"When I'm off duty. But we weren't talking about me—we were talking about you and the do-over you want God to give you."

"The do-over that will never happen, so there's no sense in talking about it?"

"What *would* you do differently, Annie? If you could go back, that is?" he pressed, because he wanted to know. Would she say that she wouldn't marry her husband? Or say that she'd have stayed home the night of the murder, made sure that Joe wasn't alone? Kept him from gambling?

"Why do you want to know, Hunter? What's in it for you?" She looked at him over her teacup, her eyes the crisp bright blue of the summer sky.

"Does there have to be something in it for me?"

"Probably. I mean, you're doing a job, and I'm

part of that. Your questions are usually all about helping you do your job better."

"This time, I just want to know."

She studied him for a moment, her gaze never wavering. "I'm not sure. I guess that I'd just be a little more honest with myself about things."

"What things?"

"You're full of questions." She smiled, but it didn't reach her eyes. "What about you? Is there anything you would change about your past?"

"No."

"That was a quick response."

"Because I'm careful in the choices I make. I want to make sure that I don't have regrets." And that he didn't give anyone else reason to have them.

"I thought I was careful, too, but I'm still here, sitting in a stranger's house, wide-awake at one in the morning because someone wants me dead."

"We don't know if there's a price on your head, Annie. We only know that someone is trying to intimidate you."

"It feels the same to me. Either way, I'm in danger, and I'm hiding out until that changes."

"Hiding out, but not with strangers. We've known each other for over a year."

"You're wrong. I haven't known you for a year. At least not in any way that matters. You may know what my favorite cookie is, but I don't know yours.

I don't know your favorite color, how many siblings you have, whether you've ever been married."

"Chocolate chip. Blue. Two. No," he said.

She offered a real smile but shook her head. "Those are easy things, Hunter. Telling me about them is like telling me that the sky is blue or the sun is shining. It's all generic and simple. The hard stuff is the stuff I want to know."

He should have ended the conversation then. Told her that it was time to go back to her room and her daughter, but it had been a long time since he'd sat next to a beautiful woman, caught a hint of her perfume in the air, felt the warmth of her body close to his and really noticed it the way he was noticing Annie.

She was a witness. There were lines he couldn't cross, lines he wouldn't cross, but sitting at a table, talking to her when she was anxious and worried… that wasn't one of them.

"Then ask the hard questions. I'll answer them," he said.

"All of them?" she laughed, grabbing another cookie and peeling the top off it.

"*Some* of them. What do you want to know?"

"Why you're a U.S. marshal."

"That's easy. The work is interesting and every case is different. I like the mental and physical challenge, too."

"So, it's not about the people?"

"It's about justice, and it's about the people. Usually not the people I'm protecting, though. Most of the time, they're criminals who are hiding from people that they've betrayed."

"I see."

"What do you see, Annie?" he asked, because he was curious. He wanted to know how he looked to her.

"That you're not what I thought you were." She frowned and wiped a wet spot off the table.

"What did you think I was?"

"Someone who didn't really care. Someone who was all about the job. All about getting the witness to trial so you could put another notch on your work belt."

"Ouch," he said mildly. He didn't blame her for thinking that. He wore the persona, and he was happy to let people believe it was a real representation of who he was.

"I'm sorry," she responded. "It's the way you act, though."

"I know."

"And you don't want to do something about it?"

"Why would I?"

"Because you're giving yourself a bad reputation."

"Like I said, most of the people I'm protecting are criminals and thugs. I'm not really all that concerned with their opinions of me."

"What about the people you work with?"

"They know me well enough to know where my heart lies."

"Where is that?" she asked, reaching for another cookie.

He snagged the package before she could grab one, pulling it out of her reach. "With the people I care about. My family. My friends. You and Sophia." He admitted the last because he thought she needed to hear it.

Her eyes widened, a small frown line appearing between her brows. "Is that why you took the cookies?"

"What?"

"Did you take the cookies because you care about my health? Because if that's the case, you can give them back. I'm not going to drown myself in a package of vanilla sandwich cookies. Tempting as it might be."

"I took the cookies because I don't think a pound of sugar is going to do much to help you fall asleep." He stood and offered his hand, pulling Annie to her feet. Heat shot up his arm, and he took a quick step back. "The prosecuting attorney rescheduled the meeting you were supposed to have yesterday. We have to be at his office at ten. You're never going to be able to drag yourself out of bed if you don't get some sleep soon."

"I won't have to drag myself. Sophia will manage to get me out of bed just fine." She rubbed her palm against her jeans, must have realized what she was doing and stopped.

He knew how she felt.

He could still feel the warmth of her skin. In all the years he'd worked as a marshal, he'd never been attracted to a witness. Never been tempted to cross the line. He'd never thought he *could* be.

He'd been wrong.

Annie was becoming a problem. If he wasn't careful, she'd become a really big one.

"But you won't be happy about it if you don't get some sleep," he responded, keeping his tone light and professional. What he was feeling had nothing to do with the job, and he wouldn't let it affect him.

"Probably not, but I'll get up anyway. I'll even be nice to Mr. Antonio and practice answering all the questions that I've already practiced answering dozens of times."

"I'm sure Antonio will appreciate it. Seeing as how you've been so difficult to work with up until this point."

She laughed. "I've been trying to hold on to my patience, but after answering the same questions so many times, I'm getting a little tired of our meetings."

"They'll be over soon," he assured her.

"I know." She smoothed her hair, rubbed the back of her neck. "Can Sophia come with us tomorrow?"

"She'll be safer here."

He thought she'd argue, but she nodded instead. "Okay. Who's staying with her?"

"Whoever you want me to get."

"Come on, Hunter." She smiled. "You don't think I'm going to believe that you don't already have someone lined up, do you?"

"Maybe you know me better than you think," he joked, but it wasn't all that funny. She shouldn't know him at all because he was supposed to be background to her life. Not part of it.

"I know that you don't leave anything to chance. So, who is it going to be?"

"Serena will be here. She's good with Sophia."

"All of you are good with her, but I'm her mother. I want to be the one to take care of her."

"She was in day care in Milwaukee. That went okay, right?" he asked even though he knew it had. He'd done the research before she'd left St. Louis, found a good neighborhood and a good day-care facility for Sophia. He'd been the only one of the team who'd known her location, and he'd kept it quiet, too, so that she could have exactly what she was describing—a feeling of security and safety.

"That was different."

"How?"

"I wasn't afraid that every time I left her, I might not return."

He hadn't thought about that. Probably because

he wasn't a father. He didn't have someone waiting for him to come home. He wouldn't be missed if he didn't return. There was something a little sad about that. Something that made him wonder if he'd made the right choice when he'd decided to opt for a career over a family.

"I'll bring you back to her. I promise you that."

"Promises are easy, Hunter. It's keeping them that's hard. You were right. I need to get some sleep. Good night." She nearly ran from the kitchen. Her feet pounded on the stairs. The floor creaked above his head.

He didn't hear the door to her room close, but he knew she'd closed it.

He dropped back into his chair, scanning the computer monitor for any sign of trouble. Nothing, and he hadn't expected there to be. No one but the immediate team knew Annie was there, and as long as Hunter had anything to do with it, no one would.

The wind howled through the eaves and rattled the windows, cold air seeping in through the windowpane. Because the house was a rental, he and Burke hadn't done much to improve the place, despite the fact that the landlord had told them they could make any changes they wanted. They'd spent so little time there, it hadn't felt important.

Now he wished they'd paid to have new windows put in, done some weatherproofing, sealed the little cracks in the old wooden panes. The upstairs rooms had once been the attic. The walls weren't insulated well. The floors were icy in the winter. Not a good place for a little girl to sleep.

Annie would keep her daughter warm. Even if that meant giving up her own blankets. That was as good an excuse as any to go upstairs. He walked up the stairs and opened the linen closet, dug through it until he found a blanket that his niece had left behind. It was small and pink with tiny flowers.

The door to Annie's room was closed. Just like he'd known it would be. He knocked softly, not sure if Annie would answer.

She'd been in a hurry to leave the kitchen.

To leave *him*.

The door opened, and Annie appeared, the black Bible clutched to her chest. He wanted to ask her why she didn't buy a new one, get something that had no connection to her husband, but it wasn't his place or his concern.

"Is everything okay?" she asked, her face pale as paper, her eyes deep blue.

"I was afraid that Sophia would get cold." He held up the blanket, and she took it.

"Thank you." She would have shut the door, but he put his hand on the wood, holding it open.

"Are you okay?" he asked.

"Why wouldn't I be?"

"Because…there's something happening between us that neither of us expected?"

"I don't—"

"You know exactly what I'm talking about." He cut her off. He didn't believe in playing games, and there was too much riding on her trusting him to ignore what they'd both felt. "How about you don't pretend otherwise?"

"All right. I won't pretend, but it doesn't mean anything."

"You're right. It doesn't, and I don't want you to do anything foolish to prove that."

"I'm not planning to."

"No matter what, Annie, you've got to stick with the plan and stay with the program. For your sake and for your daughter's."

"You don't have to keep reminding me. I know what's at stake." Her knuckles were white, her grip on the Bible and the blanket so tight, he thought she'd leave nail gauges in the leather cover and holes in the blanket.

"But do you trust me to do whatever it takes to keep you and Sophia safe?" That was the real question. The one he needed an answer to.

"I don't know, but I trust God, and this is where He's put me. Until things change, it's where I'm going to stay."

"What things?"

"How can I know, Hunter? I just know that for now, I have to stay. If that changes, I'll let you know.

Now, do you mind if I try to get some sleep? I really am exhausted."

He let go of the door, and she closed it, the lock clicking loudly in the sudden silence.

She'd said she was going to keep cooperating, but Hunter couldn't shake his concern as he walked back to the kitchen. All of her acquiescence wouldn't do any good if she suddenly decided she was finished being part of the program.

She'd be on her own then, out in the open where anyone who wanted to harm her could find her.

No bodyguards. No weapons. Just Annie and Sophia.

The thought filled him with anger, dread and a healthy dose of fear.

He paced to the living-room window and looked out into the front yard. Frozen rain coated the grass and pinged off the pavement. He'd always loved winter. The stark beauty of it reminded him that there was more to life than the hectic schedule he kept. More to living than sitting in an office or standing guard over witnesses. When he looked at snow-laden trees or the stark branches of the trees, he could see the beginnings of life and the ends of it.

Nothing lasted forever.

Winter reminded him of that.

It was in the winter that he was most likely to question the path he'd chosen. Over the years, he'd had other work offers. Local police work. Training work. He'd been offered a job as bodyguard more than once. He'd even been asked to move to Montana to help his uncle with the ranch he owned there.

He'd turned down every opportunity because St. Louis was his hometown, and U.S. Marshals work had always been his passion.

Right then, though, looking out into the wintery morning, he wasn't sure if it always would be.

TWELVE

At some point, Annie must have fallen asleep.

She didn't even remember lying down.

She'd been sitting on her bed, reading from Ephesians, the winter storm raging outside. The next thing she knew, Sophia was patting her cheek.

"Mommy! Wake up!" she cried, her sweet voice pulling Annie from the edge of sleep.

She opened her eyes. Sunlight streamed through the closed slats of the blinds and dappled Sophia's hair with gold. The storm had broken. The sun had risen.

And Annie was going to have to see Hunter again.

She wasn't all that happy about it.

Not after she'd asked him those questions the previous night. Not after he'd held her hand and she'd felt the heat of his touch zip straight into her heart.

He'd felt it, too.

And, in true Hunter fashion, he hadn't been willing to ignore it.

"Mommy!" Sophia tugged her hand, trying to pull her out of bed.

"Okay, sweetie. I'm up." She dragged herself out of bed and glanced at the clock. She had a couple of hours before she had to meet with the attorney. Plenty of time to feed Sophia and get herself ready.

She grabbed clothes from her suitcase and walked to the door. She should have just opened it, but she pressed her ear to the wood, trying to hear voices. She didn't want to face Hunter. Not yet.

"Let's go, Mommy." Sophia tugged her hand impatiently.

"Okay. Right. Let's go."

Please, don't let him be out there, she thought as she opened the door. She hadn't slept well, and she wasn't in the right frame of mind to have a conversation with anyone. Especially not Hunter.

The hall was empty, and she hurried Sophia to the bathroom. She took a quick shower and searched for a blow-dryer. She came up empty.

She toweled her hair dry and took a quick peek in the mirror. The circles under her eyes looked like the black smudges football players had under their eyes during games. Her skin was as pale as paper, her hair almost black in contrast. She'd chosen a simple black shirtdress. Usually, she loved it, but it only made her pallor more noticeable. She glanced down. It also showcased the ugly scabs on her knees. She could see them through the thick black tights she wore.

"Yikes," she murmured.

"Yikes," Sophia repeated, tugging on the skirt of Annie's dress. "Up?"

"Sure." She sighed. She could put on some makeup before she left. Maybe pull her hair back. It wasn't as if she was going to a job interview, but Mr. Antonio was constantly stressing the importance of how she presented herself during trial. Young. Demure. Respectable.

She'd always thought she was all those things, and she'd never really worried about the opinions of others, but the prosecuting attorney and his team were worried about Joe. He'd been a gambler, a liar. He'd borrowed money from people who were part of a crime syndicate that had been responsible for murders, robberies and drug running.

Annie had to be the antithesis of all of that because her testimony against the men who'd murdered Joe was the keystone to the prosecutor's case. Without it, there was a very good chance that one or both of the men would walk away free.

She lifted Sophia, her palms sore and raw. A good reminder of her foolishness. She should have trusted Hunter, and if she hadn't been able to do that, she should have trusted God.

He was in control. Not the prosecuting attorney. Not the marshals. Not whoever was trying to scare Annie into silence. She'd forgotten that for a while, but a long, sleepless night reading her Bible and praying had reminded her of where her strength and hope lay.

She just had to keep that in mind as she went through the day.

The house was silent as she walked downstairs and into the living room. The lights were off, the curtains closed. She braced herself as she walked to the kitchen. Burke should be pulling his shift by now, and Hunter should be sleeping or getting ready to escort her to the lawyer's office.

Hopefully.

Because she wasn't in the right frame of mind to face him.

She walked into the kitchen, nearly sagging with relief when she saw Burke, his head bent over what looked like a dismantled high chair.

"Morning," he said without looking up. "Coffee is ready. Serena dropped off some stuff for breakfast. Check the fridge."

"Thanks."

"I'll have this contraption put together in a few minutes, if you want to wait to feed Sophia." He snapped a piece of plastic into place and set the high chair upright. He had a slimmer build than Hunter, his muscles less defined beneath the white dress shirt he wore. "Hunter should be down soon. I think he said you're leaving at nine."

"The meeting isn't until ten." She opened the fridge, snagging Sophia's hands just before she pulled eggs from the side shelf.

"You're meeting at a friend of Antonio's instead of his office. It's too risky to do anything else."

"Risky?" She grabbed a yogurt and some blueberries and carried them to the table.

"The closer we get to trial, the higher the risk. Hunter doesn't want to take any chances. None of us do." He set the high chair into place near the table, brushed his hands on his black slacks. "There you go. Perfect."

"Thanks, Burke," she said, setting Sophia into the chair and strapping her in. "This is going to make feeding her a lot easier."

"Anything for you, doll," he said with a wink.

She ignored the flirtation.

Even before she'd married Joe, she hadn't been much for it. She'd wanted to settle down, not play the field.

A box of Cheerios sat on the counter. She poured a few onto the tray of the high chair, cut a banana into pieces that Sophia could enjoy. They could share the yogurt. Annie wasn't all that excited about eating. Too many cookies in the middle of the night.

"You were up late last night," Burke said as she grabbed a spoon and settled into the chair beside Sophia.

"Yes," she responded. She didn't want to go into the reasons why.

"I heard you talking to Hunter."

Her heart jumped, but she didn't rise to the bait.

Whatever he'd heard was none of his business. "I'm sorry if we woke you."

"I was already awake. I heard you go downstairs, and I wanted to make sure you came back up."

"I did." She spooned yogurt into Sophia's mouth, her appetite completely gone. This wasn't a conversation she wanted to have, but it seemed as though she was going to.

"I know. Listen," he said, taking the chair beside her and leaning toward her, his body relaxed, his expression neutral. "If you're uncomfortable with Hunter escorting you to Antonio's meeting today, I can do it."

"Why would I be?"

"Just a feeling I have that there's something going on between the two of you."

"You're wrong. There isn't."

"Not yet. But what's going to happen in the next two weeks? Are you still going to be able to keep a professional distance between you? You've got to admit, the circumstances you're in breed reliance and that can lead to feelings that a person normally wouldn't have."

She knew her cheeks were the color of ripe tomatoes, but she looked straight into his eyes. No way was she going to let him continue in the direction he was headed. "The only thing it's breeding is a need for this trial to end so that I can get back to my life."

He studied her for a long moment and then

shrugged. "You're lying to yourself if you really think that."

"I'm not—"

Footsteps sounded on the stairs, the old floorboards groaning.

"That's Hunter," Burke said. "If you want me to play escort today, now's the time to say it."

She didn't have time to respond before Hunter walked into the room. Fresh from the shower, his hair still damp, his face newly shaven, he looked better than the first spring flower after a long winter.

Her pulse jumped, and she looked away. She realized that Burke was staring at her and spooned more yogurt into Sophia's mouth.

"What's going on?" Hunter asked.

"I was just offering to escort Annie to the meeting with Antonio today."

"The plan is already worked out. There's no need to change it," Hunter responded as he crossed the room and poured coffee into a mug. He smelled like soap and some spicy aftershave that made Annie think of long hikes in a pine forest and rafting trips on the river. It made her think of the vices that he'd said he'd get her hooked on, and made her remember the way he'd looked when he'd said there was something between them that neither could deny.

He'd been right about that.

She couldn't deny it, but she didn't have to acknowledge it, either.

"I think that maybe there is," Burke said, and Annie tensed.

"Okay. Go ahead. Spill it." Hunter sat next to Annie, his arm brushing hers. Her muscles tightened in response, every nerve in her body demanding that she lean closer.

"You two are getting too close, Hunter. I think it's time to put some distance between you."

"We're not—" Annie started to say, but Hunter cut her off.

"Have I ever been anything other than professional in my job?" he asked without a hint of emotion in his voice.

"There's a first time for everything," Burke replied. "So, how about you tell me where Antonio's friend lives and let me escort Annie there? You take the day off and get some fresh air. Clear your head so you can think straight again."

"I'm thinking plenty straight, and what I'm thinking is that we have a plan in place and there's no reason to change it."

"I'm looking out for your better interest, Hunter. I think you know that."

"The only person you need to worry about is Annie. Last night, we agreed that the meeting site was going to be on a need-to-know basis. Only one person needs to know where it's taking place. Three if you count Antonio and his friend. Until we find our leak, this is the way things have to be."

"Yeah, but—"

"You came up with the idea, Burke. Not me."

"That was before…" His voice trailed off and he shook his head.

"What?" Hunter pressed.

"Nothing. I just thought I'd help you out, but if you don't want it, I'm cool with taking the morning off." Burke switched gears easily, his hard expression changing to one of easy acceptance.

Annie wasn't sure he was as content with the outcome of the argument as he pretended to be, but both men let the subject drop.

"Are you ready to head out once Serena gets here?" Hunter turned his attention to Annie, his dark eyes blazing.

"Yes. How long do you think we'll be gone?"

"A couple of hours," he replied, taking a sip of coffee and grabbing a handful of blueberries from the container.

"I should probably make Sophia's lunch and put it in the fridge. That way Serena won't have to worry—"

"Too late," Burke broke in. "She's pulling into the driveway. Better get your purse so you can get out of here."

She almost argued, but the two men were staring each other down, and she honestly didn't want to hear them argue about her or the case.

"I'll be right back, Sophia," she said, dropping a kiss on her daughter's head and hurrying from the room.

Hunter waited until the sound of Annie's footsteps faded away, then he turned to Burke.

"What was that all about?" he demanded, glad to see that Burke had the decency to look embarrassed.

"I'm just trying to protect you, Hunter. You're letting this case get to you."

"The way you let the Simmons case get to you?" Burke had fallen hard for the witness in that case. He hadn't broken protocol, but he'd come close, and they'd both known it.

When Audrey Simmons finally testified against her ex-husband, she'd gone deep into witness protection. As far as Hunter knew, that had been the end of things. He was sure that Burke would have liked more, though.

"That is exactly why I'm trying to protect you," Burke admitted. "I don't want you to make my mistake."

"Don't worry. Things are under control."

"I hope so," Burke muttered as Serena walked in through the laundry room.

"Everything okay in here?" she asked, her gaze jumping from Hunter to Burke and back again.

"Fine. We were just discussing today's logistics."

"Oh, I thought maybe you were talking about the new guy." She poured herself some coffee. She'd chosen jeans and a T-shirt for babysitting duty and had pulled her hair into a ponytail.

"You mean Da…" Burke's voice trailed off.

"Yes. I mean Daniel's replacement," she said as if it didn't bother her.

Hunter knew it did. "We haven't made any decisions about who that's going to be yet, Serena. Once we do, you'll be the first to know."

"You're considering Colton Philips, aren't you?"

"His name has come up." Colton had been working for the marshals for a while. He had a reputation for getting jobs done. He also had a reputation for doing things his way.

"And?" she demanded.

"I'm going to talk to him, but I don't think he'll be a good fit. He's moved around a lot. Seems to have a reputation for skirting the rules."

"Definitely not your kind of team member," Burke said, his shoulder against the wall, his arms crossed. He still didn't seem all that happy. Maybe *he* had a thing for Annie. Something that went beyond just natural concern for a witness.

If so, Hunter couldn't say he blamed him.

He still wasn't going to switch the plan. "Would he be *your* kind?"

"No," Burke admitted. "I may do things my own

way sometimes, but I'm not into the maverick type. They're not good for team building."

"Agreed. I'll keep you guys posted." He glanced at his watch. "I need to get Annie and head out."

He was halfway through the living room when the floor at the top of the stairs creaked. He knew Annie was on her way down, but he walked to the staircase anyway.

She'd hooked her purse over her shoulder and pulled her hair into a high ponytail that brushed her nape. Head down, eyes focused on a piece of paper she was holding, she seemed oblivious to his presence.

"Ready?" he asked, and she jumped.

"I didn't realize you were there," she said with a little laugh.

"I wasn't trying to make a secret of it. What are you studying? Notes for the trial?"

"No. I'm prepared for that. I'm just…" Her cheeks went three shades of red, and she folded the paper and shoved it into her purse.

"What?"

"Reminding myself why I'm doing this."

"Going to talk to Steven Antonio?"

"Testifying."

He didn't say anything as he led her into the kitchen.

He was curious, though.

He wanted to know what was on the paper.

He waited while she kissed Sophia goodbye and gave Serena instructions that probably wouldn't be followed. Serena would do her own thing with Sophia, and that would be fine. As long as the little girl was safe and happy, Hunter didn't see any harm in that.

Once she was finished, he cupped her elbow and led her into the garage. He unlocked the door to the SUV, and she slid into the passenger seat. He was uncomfortably aware of her presence. He took his time getting into the SUV, letting the cold garage cool his blood and refocus his thoughts.

He had a job to do, and he needed to get it done. Until he did, nothing else could matter.

THIRTEEN

Annie leaned her head against the seat and closed her eyes. Maybe if she kept them closed, Hunter would make the trip in silence.

She should have known better.

"So, what was on the piece of paper you stuck in your purse?" he asked before they even pulled out of the garage.

"A list."

"Of reasons why you're testifying?"

"Yes." As silly as it seemed, she'd written them down before she'd left St. Louis, and she'd carried them with her to Milwaukee and back again because she'd wanted to remember why she'd agreed to work with the marshals.

"What were they?"

She didn't really feel like talking about them. She didn't want to think about the horrible hours she'd spent after Joe's murder. Didn't want to remember how desperate she'd been to find Sophia or how scared she'd been that she never would.

She'd been at the hospital, dressed in a stranger's clothes because hers had been taken as evidence, waiting and praying that the police would find Sophia and that she was okay.

When the door had opened and a police officer had walked in with Sophia, she'd almost passed out with relief. She'd stayed with her parents for the next week, huddled in her old room, terrified and grief-stricken.

Eventually, she'd identified the two men she'd seen in her kitchen. She'd have known either of them anywhere. John Fiske's pinched weasellike face. Luke Saunders's dragon tattoo dancing along his forearm as he'd pointed the gun in her direction.

She shuddered.

The police had arrested them both, and she'd been approached by Hunter. He'd asked her to testify and promised to keep her safe until trial. It had seemed like the right thing to do until a couple of days before she was supposed to leave town.

Then she'd doubted her choice, wondered if maybe she'd be better off staying in St. Louis. That was when she'd written the list.

It seemed like a lifetime ago, and she felt like a different person. Not the young and happy woman she'd been before Joe's murder. A jaded, older version of herself.

The reasons she'd written a year ago seemed so naive, so simplistic.

"So, you're not going to share?" Hunter asked as he backed out of the garage and pulled onto the quiet street.

"There's nothing to share, really."

"Which means there is plenty to share." He glanced in the rearview mirror, probably making sure they weren't being followed.

She resisted the urge to turn around and see for herself.

"I wanted to do it for Joe. I thought he'd been in the wrong place at the wrong time. I wanted justice for him because it felt so unfair that he died for nothing."

"It still is unfair, Annie. Just because your husband borrowed money from the wrong people doesn't mean that he deserved to die," Hunter said gently.

She knew he was right, but things had felt different since she'd found out about Joe's secret life. It wasn't that she thought he deserved what he'd gotten. It was just that she kept thinking that he could have prevented it. "I know, but he was part of the tragedy that happened to him. A knowing participant in the events that led to his murder. That doesn't mean he deserved it, but it means that it could have been prevented." She sighed and looked out the window. "That's what I can't forget."

"And what you can't forgive him for?"

"I've forgiven him, but I can't seem to forget that

all the plans and dreams and goals we had died with him. I can't stop thinking that if he'd just been doing the things he'd said he was, he wouldn't be dead, and we'd still be raising Sophia together."

"Do you really think that?" he asked as he pulled onto the highway and headed toward the suburbs. "Because the way I read the Bible, we each have a certain number of days. Once those days are up, our lives on earth are over. There's nothing we can do to stretch that number out, so we've got to live the best way we can every day that we have."

He was right, but it was so much easier to think about other things. Like Hunter with a leather Bible in his tan hands. "You read the Bible?"

"You sound surprised."

"I…guess I am." He'd been accompanying her to church every Sunday since she'd returned to St. Louis, but she hadn't realized that attending meant anything to him.

"Why?"

"Because you're all about facts and figures and rules."

"And that means I can't have faith?" he asked with a short laugh.

"No, but you've never mentioned it."

"It isn't something I talk about to witnesses."

"You're talking about it now," she pointed out.

"Because the subject came up." He sighed. "And because I've been thinking about it a lot more lately.

I guess that's what happens when you go to church every Sunday."

"You weren't doing that before?"

"Sleeping seemed a little more important than getting up early to attend services." He offered a wry smile. "Thanks to you, I've learned the error of my ways. But we weren't talking about me and my mistakes. We were talking about Joe and how hard it is for you to forgive him."

"It isn't hard," she protested, but it was.

No matter how many times she told herself that she'd forgiven Joe, she couldn't let go of the pain. He'd lied to her, betrayed her trust and then he'd been killed.

It was all tied up together in a knot of unhappiness that spent most of its time sitting right in the center of Annie's chest. Some days, it was so heavy and tight she could barely breathe.

"It *is* hard, Annie, because you were supposed to have an entire lifetime with someone who promised to love and honor you. Instead you're raising your daughter by yourself, spending your days locked away because you're afraid for your life. You took vows before God. You lived by them, but Joe didn't, and now you're left cleaning up the mess he left behind."

He was right.

She couldn't deny it.

She stared out the window, watching as trees and houses whizzed by, hot tears burning her eyes.

"It's okay to admit that you're angry," Hunter said quietly.

"What good will that do? Joe will still be dead. I'll still be alone raising a little girl who will never know her father." She sounded pitiful, and she hated that. She'd always tried to maintain an attitude of thanksgiving, but over the past year that had been difficult.

She knew that God had a purpose and plan for everything. Even the hard things.

That didn't make it any easier to go through.

"You're not alone. You have me and my team." He patted her thigh, his hand warm through her cotton dress. Even after he pulled away, the warmth of his touch lingered.

"That's even more pitiful than being alone." She kept her voice light, tried hard not to let any of her feelings seep into the words. There was no place for them in her life. Not then. Probably not ever.

"It's not pitiful, and neither are you," he said as if he'd read her mind, knew exactly what she'd been thinking.

"At this moment, Hunter, you are the closest thing I have to a friend and, aside from Sophia, the closest thing I have to family. If that's not ridiculously pitiful, I don't know what is. So, how about we change the subject?"

"To what?"

"Did the police find anything at the apartment complex yesterday?"

"A homemade explosive device. Small. The car it was in was parked away from other vehicles," Hunter replied. He'd wondered how long it would take before she changed the subject.

"So, whoever planted it didn't want to hurt anyone?"

"It's hard to say."

"But you have an opinion about it, I'm sure." She tapped her fingers on her thigh. The same thigh he'd patted. Unintentionally. He hadn't been thinking about the job, protocol, right and wrong. He'd just been thinking about Annie and how hard things had been for her since her husband's murder.

He also hadn't been thinking that that simple touch would warm his blood, leave him wanting more.

His fingers tightened around the steering wheel. "My opinion," he said, trying to refocus his thoughts, "is that the bomb was a distraction. The perp didn't intend to hurt anyone with it. He detonated it remotely. Which means he was either waiting somewhere close by, watching for you to exit the apartment, or he had someone else close enough to do it for him."

"What about your security footage? You'd been watching the entire building, right?"

"Most of it. We have footage of the car entering the parking garage about an hour before you left the apartment. The perp got out and walked away. He was wearing a hat and scarf. Not unusual this time of year, but certainly good for hiding someone who doesn't want to be identified. Obviously, he knew when your appointment with Antonio was, and he was waiting for you to leave for it."

"Why not just shoot me when I walked outside, then?" she asked, her muscles trembling slightly.

"Too easy for him to be seen. He was probably hoping to take a shot as we were leaving. Either that or he was just using more scare tactics and never intended to attack you physically."

"If that's the case, it worked. I'm scared." She turned to look out the side window, her ponytail swinging slightly as the SUV bounced over a rut in the road.

"Don't be. The bomb was an act of desperation. The perp might have known where you were, but he still wasn't able to get to you."

Saunders and Fiske were small-time thugs. Their criminal records were rife with petty crime and drug dealings. Nothing big. Even considering the money Joe owed to the crime organization they were affiliated with, it was surprising that they'd crossed the line into murder. Someone else was calling the shots. More than likely, someone both men were afraid of.

They weren't saying, though.

They'd been silent on the motive for murder, refusing to answer questions during the year that they'd been awaiting trial. That wasn't going to affect the outcome of the case.

Thanks to Annie.

She was the perfect witness. Intelligent. Hardworking. Focused. A law-abiding citizen who'd never even gotten a parking ticket. She'd spent her life playing by the rules. The prosecuting team had left no stone unturned. Antonio had looked for even the smallest thing because he'd wanted to make sure the defense wouldn't be able to plant doubt in the minds of the jury.

There'd been nothing.

Annie would go to trial with a pristine past, her memory of her husband's murder clear and crisp in her mind. She'd seen everything. Saunders pulling the trigger. Joe falling. Blood splattering on the white cabinets and the floor. John Fiske hovering in the back doorway, urging Saunders to hurry up. The gun pointed at her head, misfiring and clattering onto the floor.

Hunter had heard the story dozens of times over the past month. Annie had told it the same way every time, her voice shaking a little, her face pale. He'd detached himself from her fear and pain because he'd wanted no part of it. Staying focused on protecting her meant not giving in to the compassion and sympathy he had for her.

She needed more than that, though. She *deserved* more.

She'd said it herself—he was all she had. The closest thing to friends and family she had.

He pulled on to a cul-de-sac lined with oversize houses and drove to the end, where a brick two-story hulked over a pristine yard. The driveway was three cars wide to match the garage. Antonio's black Cadillac was already parked in one of the spots.

"Is this it?" Annie asked as he parked next to Antonio's car. "The house is huge!"

"Looks like twenty people could live in it comfortably," he agreed, but his mind wasn't on the conversation or on the house. It was on Annie. On everything she'd been through, everything he'd shoved to the back of his mind because he didn't want to see her as anything other than a job he had to do.

Something had changed.

He'd acknowledged that to himself, but he wasn't quite sure what to do about it. He knew what he *had* to do. Get her into the house, let her be questioned for hours in preparation for trial.

He touched her shoulder, his fingers curving around narrow bone and firm muscle. "When this is over, when the trial ends and Fiske and Saunders are in jail—"

"*If* they are. We don't know what the outcome is going to be."

"*I* know. Your testimony is flawless, and the case is airtight," he assured her, worried about the dark circles under her eyes and the pallid cast to her skin. Despite the cookies she loved so much, she was still losing weight, her cheekbones gaunt, her eyes hollow. The year of hiding had taken its toll. He wanted to take away the stress and anxiety, give her something that would make her smile.

"I hope you're right, Hunter. I just…" She bit her lower lip, her gaze dark and troubled. "I want to get my life back. I want to go to the park with Sophia and know that we're going to be safe. I want to go for a jog, buy groceries, drive to work without looking over my shoulder. I want all the things that I took for granted before."

"You'll have them."

She sighed. "You want to hear something funny?"

"Sure." But he had a feeling it wasn't going to be funny.

"I've never really liked St. Louis. I always wanted to live somewhere rural. Like Wyoming or Montana or North Dakota. I wanted a lot of wide-open space where my kids could run and play in clean, fresh air."

"I know a place like that. I spent every summer there for the first eighteen years of my life." Because his father had been too busy to take a vacation, and his mother had been too overwhelmed to plan a vacation for her kids, they'd flown to Montana to visit her family every summer. Hunter's uncle Nate had taken all three kids under his wing, but Hunter had been the one who loved the ranch, the fresh air, the clean crisp air the most.

He'd almost moved to Billings after he'd graduated college, taken a job in law enforcement there, but the job with the marshals had opened up. It was an opportunity he'd been hoping for, and he'd taken it.

"I spent every summer at the St. Louis library," Annie said. "Reading about all the places I wanted to visit. Milwaukee wasn't one of them."

She sounded so disgusted that he chuckled, brushing a strand of hair from her cheek without realizing what he was doing.

He pulled back, clenching his hands into fists to keep from touching her again. "Sorry about that. I didn't get to make the choice about where you were going when you left St. Louis."

"It's a nice enough place, but after this is over, I'm going to go somewhere else."

"Yeah?" He got out of the SUV, walked around to her door and helped her out. "Where do you want to go?"

"Somewhere safe. Somewhere where Sophia can run around and keep pets and enjoy being a little girl."

"I'll make sure you get to go where you want

this time, so think about it between now and the trial," he said. The cul-de-sac was still and quiet, but he hurried her to the porch, the hair on the back of his neck standing on end. He wanted her inside and safe.

"Thanks."

"The other thing I'm going to make sure you get is a visit with your parents before you leave town."

"Really?" She stopped, her foot on the first step of a wide front porch, sunlight glinting in her dark hair. Threads of gold and red were woven through the dark strands, the burnished highlights natural and even more beautiful because they were.

"Yes."

"I thought I wasn't going to be able to see them while I was here."

"Once the trial is over, I'll try to arrange something. It should be safe for you to spend a few hours with your folks." He cupped her elbow, urging her up the stairs. The danger might be minimal, but the sooner he got her inside the house, the happier he'd be.

The door opened before they reached it, Steven Antonio motioning for them to enter.

"Glad you could make it for the meeting," he said, his narrow face creased in a smile that didn't quite meet his eyes. "We'll be in the office in the back of the house. Bud made coffee."

"Bud?" Hunter asked.

"Hollingsworth. He heard about security being breached at the safe house and knew I'd been planning to meet with Annie. We were at lunch yesterday discussing the case. He offered his place. It seemed like a better idea than bringing Annie to my place or my office."

The news was a surprise, but not an unpleasant one. A retired U.S. marshal, Bud was a go-to person when difficult cases arose. As a matter of fact, Hunter wouldn't mind discussing the case with him. He might have some ideas about who the leak might be or, at least, where it might be originating. "Is Bud around?"

"Right here!" Bud called from a room to the left of the door. A second later, he appeared in the doorway, his khaki pants and blue polo more casual than any outfit Hunter had ever seen him in.

"How are you, Hunter? Annie?" he asked with a warm smile. "I heard there was some trouble yesterday."

"Everyone is fine, but you're right. We're having a problem," Hunter admitted.

"A leak, if the way the safe houses are being found is any indication. Want to hash it out while Steven and Annie talk?"

Hunter hesitated, realizing that if Annie were any other witness, he'd be fine with Bud's plan.

"Sure," he said, giving Annie a quick smile. "Unless you'd rather I stay with you."

"I'll be fine. Thanks."

"All right. Let's get this show on the road, then," Steven said, taking Annie's arm and leading her down the hall.

She seemed reluctant to go, her muscles stiff and tense, her footsteps heavy as she walked into a room to the left of the door.

Hunter wanted to go after her, wanted it more than he wanted to follow the rules and stick to protocol. Wanted it not because he thought she wouldn't be safe, but because he thought she needed him.

Even if she wasn't willing to admit it.

FOURTEEN

By the time Annie answered the last of Steven Antonio's questions, her head was pounding so hard she thought she was going to be sick.

Not enough sleep and too much worry. That was the problem. The only solution was getting through the trial.

She sipped lukewarm coffee while Steven glanced through his notes, deep lines grooved into his forehead. He probably worried a lot and spent too many nights bent over files and notes.

She couldn't fault him for being meticulous and thorough. She couldn't hold it against him for wanting to make sure every detail had been covered, every possibility discussed.

But she was tired. They'd been there two hours, and she was ready to go home to Sophia.

Home?

She and Sophia didn't have one anymore.

Not yet, but if Hunter was telling the truth, she could choose any place in the United States to settle down in. She could rent a little house on acreage in a small community where everyone knew everyone.

She could have the things she'd wanted when she'd met Joe but had given up because his dreams were so different from hers. Of course, she'd have it all as a single mother. She'd never expected that, hadn't planned for it.

She'd never wanted to raise a child alone, but she'd make it work. Just the way she'd made the past year work. One day at a time.

"Okay, Annie," Steven said. "Looks like we're all set. I don't think I'll need to see you again until the day before the trial."

"That's great!" she exclaimed.

He smiled, running his hand over thinning brown hair. "I'm glad you're not disappointed."

"It's not that I don't enjoy our meetings—"

He laughed and shook his head. "Better not start lying now, Annie. Your reputation is stellar, and we want to keep it that way until the trial."

"Okay." She smiled, relieved that the meeting had drawn to an end. "It's not that I have anything against you. I'd just prefer to be with my daughter. Especially with everything that's been going on."

"Understandable, and I think keeping you in one place rather than having you transported to more meetings is the best way to keep you safe." He stacked a sheaf of papers and placed it in a folder.

"If you'll wait here, I'll see if Bud and Hunter are finished."

"All right." She stood as he exited the room, afraid if she sat in silence she'd fall asleep.

She wasn't sure who Bud Hollingsworth was, but his house was gorgeous, the office large with floor-to-ceiling windows that probably looked out over the front and side yards. She couldn't know for sure, because heavy curtains blocked the view. She didn't dare pull them back and take a look outside.

Faint voices drifted into the room, but they didn't seem to be coming closer. She walked to a large shelf filled with books, each one turned with the spine out, all of them organized from tallest to shortest. No photos of family or friends, but the place had a homey feel. She wouldn't have minded having an office with shelves of books and a big desk.

She wouldn't have minded just having the little house that she and Joe had chosen together, the tiny kitchen with the peeling linoleum.

For some reason, thinking about that made her eyes burn and the knot in her chest grow tighter. Once the trial was over, she'd move on. All the things that she and Joe had created together would become distant memories. She tried to remember their wedding day, the way he'd looked as she'd walked toward him down the aisle, but she only had a vague impression of sandy brown hair and a thin face, a tuxedo and a church filled with well-wishers.

"We're finished, Annie. Ready to go?" Hunter appeared in the doorway, his eyes deep chocolate-brown, his face cut in hard angles and plains. If she closed her eyes, she knew she could picture him perfectly.

She swallowed down a wave of grief and guilt. It had been only a year, and she'd already forgotten so much about Joe. The most vivid thing she remembered was his death.

And his lies.

"Are you okay?" Hunter stepped into the room.

"I'm fine," she lied, because she couldn't tell him why she wasn't. Not without saying more than she wanted to.

"You don't look fine."

"Thanks." She grabbed her coat from the back of the chair she'd hung it on.

He took it from her hands, helped her into it, his knuckles brushing her nape. "Let me rephrase that. You look beautiful but tired."

"Thanks. Again," she murmured, her cheeks suddenly hot, her heart racing a little too fast.

"It's just an observation." He pulled the edges of her ponytail out from the collar of the coat. "No need for thanks. Come on. Let's get out of here." He pressed a hand to the small of her back. Even though she was sure she shouldn't be able to, she could feel the warmth of his palm and the gentle pressure from each of his fingers.

For a year, Hunter had been in the periphery of her life. He'd called the shots, made the decisions, told her where to be and when. Other than that, he'd kept his distance.

He wasn't keeping his distance any longer. She couldn't deny her heart's quick thrum of happiness at the thought. She also couldn't deny that guilt that stabbed through her.

Joe had been dead for only a year.

How was it possible that she was looking at another man? How was it possible that she was finding him attractive?

Not just his looks, either.

The way he cared for Sophia. The way he cared for *her*. He was always kind, always willing to go the extra mile to make sure they were comfortable and happy. He'd been there for her through some of the toughest times she'd ever lived through. She knew he'd just been doing his job, but things would have been a lot worse without him there.

A schoolgirl's crush, that was what she had.

And it was downright embarrassing.

She cast a quick look in his direction.

He seemed oblivious to her thoughts.

She hoped that he was.

Feeling a quick zing of physical attraction was one thing. A full-blown case of puppy lo…

"Enough!" she whispered. She did not have a case of puppy love. Not even close. What she had was a splitting headache and a brain that was functioning on three hours of sleep.

"What was that?" Hunter asked, one dark eyebrow raised in question.

"Just talking to myself."

"Do you make a habit of that?"

"Only on days when I've been driven crazy by repetitive questions and memorized answers."

He laughed, pushing open the front door and motioning for her to wait while he walked onto the porch.

"We're good. Come on." He grabbed her hand and hurried to his SUV. She climbed in quickly, more to put some distance between them than because she was afraid that danger might be lurking nearby.

She thought he would close the door, but he leaned in, his face a couple of inches from hers. "For right now, we're just going to concentrate on getting you to trial. We'll worry about the rest after it's over."

"The rest of what?"

"This." He touched her cheek, his finger trailing along the hollow and stopping just short of her lips.

Her breath caught. Her heart skipped a beat.

She wanted to close the distance between them almost as much as she wanted to run from the way Hunter made her feel.

He closed the door, leaving her pulse thrumming and her thoughts racing. It took him way too little time to round the SUV and get into the driver's seat.

She tensed, not sure what he was going to say. Not sure what she *should* say.

"How did the meeting go?" he asked, the question so mundane, so typical of every conversation they'd ever had that she wondered if she'd imagined his other words.

"The same as always. Steven says that we probably won't have to meet again until the day before the trial." She hoped he couldn't hear the slight tremor in her voice.

"That's good news. The more hidden we can keep you, the more likely our chances are of getting you to trial without another incident."

"Is that what you call a beheaded doll and a bomb? 'Incidents'?" she asked, doing her best to act just as fine as he seemed.

She wasn't, though.

She felt shaken and unsure, every thought she'd had about schoolgirl crushes and puppy love making her want to crawl under the seat and hide.

Which was silly and childish.

Being attracted to Hunter wasn't a crime.

But it might get her into way more trouble than she wanted.

"Do you have another word for it?" he asked as he backed out of the driveway.

"'Intimidation tactics'? 'Attacks'?"

"Those work," he conceded, shooting a quick smile in her direction. He had a fantastic smile.

The kind that changed his face from stern and un-approachable to warm and inviting.

She looked away, focusing her attention on the world outside the window.

"Did you mean what you said about me visiting my parents, Hunter?" she asked. Anything to keep the conversation going, keep silence from taking hold of them. She didn't want to sit quietly the entire trip back, thinking about what he'd said, what she'd felt, what it all meant.

"I told you that I did."

"Can I tell them?" Her parents would be ecstatic. It had been a year since she'd seen them. In that time, Sophia had gone from being a baby to being a toddler. Hunter had agreed to forward photos on a couple of occasions, but pictures weren't the same as seeing someone in person.

"You know the rules. No contact with family members as long as you're in the program."

"I know the rules. I'm just getting tired of fol-lowing them."

"It's only—"

"A couple more weeks." She sighed. "Trust me. I know. I've had the date memorized for months. How did *your* meeting go?"

"Good. Bud is going to put his ear to the ground, listen for any rumors. He worked for the marshals for years, and he has contacts all over the city. It's possible someone on the streets has heard rumors about a rogue marshal. If so, Bud is the guy who can find out."

"He's retired?"

"Supposedly."

"What does that mean?"

"It means he retired a year ago, but we call him in when we have particularly tough cases. Like yours."

"I thought mine was pretty straightforward."

"It was until someone found you. Twice." He merged onto the highway, the sun high overhead, the sky gray-blue and dotted with clouds. A beautiful day. She wanted to take Sophia to a park, put her in a baby swing and listen to her squeal in delight. She wanted to take her to the grocery store, let her pretend to steer the little car cart while she shopped for groceries.

What she didn't want to do was go back to Hunter and Burke's place.

She rubbed her forehead, trying to ease the terrible ache behind her eyes.

"Headache?" Hunter asked, resting his hand on her nape.

"Yes."

"I'm not surprised. Your muscles are coiled like a rattlesnake ready to strike." He kneaded the tight muscles at the base of her neck.

It felt so good, she almost closed her eyes, leaned back into his hand. Gave herself over to another person's touch.

She stiffened, forcing herself not to melt.

"Relax," he said. "If you're tense, it defeats the whole purpose of a neck massage."

"I am relaxed."

"Right."

"I *am*."

"Then why are your hands fisted, and why do you look like you're ready to jump out of the SUV?" His hand dropped away, and she told herself she was glad, but she wasn't sure it was true.

"I guess I've been tense for so many months, I've forgotten what relaxed feels like." *That* was the truth.

"I'm sorry, Annie. I wish things were different." He glanced in the rearview mirror and frowned.

"What's wrong?"

"Probably nothing."

"Then why do you look like it's something?" She craned her neck to see what was behind them. The highway was filled with commuter traffic. Trucks. Cars. Vans. She didn't know what she was looking for, but she scanned the lanes of vehicles anyway.

"You're going to get a crick in your neck," Hunter said calmly. He didn't sound anxious, but he never did. There could be an army of men with submachine guns chasing them, and Annie thought he'd sound and look as cool as a cucumber.

"I wouldn't have to risk it if you'd just tell me what's going on."

Hunter mumbled something she couldn't quite hear and shook his head.

"What?" she asked, still watching the traffic behind them.

"When are you going to start trusting me, Annie?" he responded, and the tone of his voice pulled her attention from the road and to him.

He was looking straight ahead, eyes focused on the road, hands tight around the steering wheel. His profile was austere, his cheekbones high and sharp, his hair just brushing the collar of his shirt. In the year she'd known him, she couldn't think of one time when he'd betrayed her trust or failed to follow through on something he'd said he would do. The one time that she'd been sure he was lying, she'd been wrong.

If anyone she knew was trustworthy, it was Hunter.

"I do trust you."

"Then why are you watching traffic?"

"Because..." Why? He'd asked a valid question, and she couldn't think of an answer. Except that she really *didn't* trust him. Not completely. Despite everything he'd done, she couldn't quite believe that he only had her and Sophia's best interest at heart.

"Exactly," he muttered, and she felt like a horrible person. Or, at least, a horrible witness or client or whatever it was that Hunter referred to her as when he talked about work.

"It isn't that I don't trust you. It's just that I've been doing everything on my own for a year, and it's hard to just let go and let someone else do them for me."

"You haven't been doing things on your own. I've been in the background, making sure you were in safe locations, keeping my eye on the people who might want to harm you, offering you advice on how to stay secure and move under the radar. Have you forgotten that?"

"No, and I'm grateful for it. But when push comes to shove, I'm still the one who is responsible for Sophia."

"True, but I don't think that your need to protect your daughter is the real issue." He glanced in the rearview mirror again and exited the interstate.

"And I'm sure you're going to tell me what the real issue is."

"Why not? We've got a little time," he said.

If he'd been anyone else, she'd have thought he was joking, but he looked dead serious, his jaw tight, his expression hard.

"Well?" she demanded. "Go ahead. Tell me why I don't trust you."

"You judge every man according to what your husband did. He lied, so we all must lie. He betrayed your trust, so obviously, we all are going to. You're so busy trying to make sure you're not fooled again that you're putting up walls that don't need to be there, protecting yourself from things you don't need to be protected from."

That's not true, she wanted to say.

But it *was.*

"Nothing to say to that?" he asked quietly, the hard edge gone from his voice.

Maybe he regretted his words, but they'd been said, and he couldn't take them back. Besides, he was right. She *was* trying to protect herself and Sophia, guarding her heart because she was afraid to have it broken again.

"No," she finally said.

"At least you're not denying it."

"I'm not going to change it, either. I have a right to the way I feel, Hunter. I have a responsibility to myself and Sophia. It is *my* job to make sure that she's secure and safe. Not yours or anyone else's. That has nothing to do with what Joe did."

"It has everything to do with it. If he hadn't died, you'd be living in the little house on Pine Street. You'd be tripping over the loose piece of linoleum in the laundry room every day and cooking on the stove that only had two working burners. You'd be tutoring in the evening and babysitting during the day, and doing everything you could to make something pleasant out of your life."

"So what?" she snapped, angry because he'd made her former life sound petty and small. "I liked my life. I loved my little house. I enjoyed tutoring and babysitting."

"Exactly," he agreed. "And Joe took it all away. Like I said earlier, you have every right to be angry. But you can't paint every man with the broad stroke of your husband's betrayal. If you do, you may miss out on some great things."

She stared out the window, her head throbbing with every heartbeat, her eyes burning with tears. She was angry, and no matter how many times she'd prayed that God would help her forgive and move on, she couldn't seem to do either. Not completely.

She pressed her forehead against cool glass and closed her eyes. Hunter was right, but she didn't know how to do things differently. She didn't know how to lower her guard and let herself go back to being the way she'd been before. Trusting and young and filled with dreams. She wasn't sure she wanted to go back to being that person. She might be jaded, but she was stronger. She might have learned some hard lessons, but she'd grown wiser from them.

The car stopped, and she opened her eyes, surprised to see trees and playground equipment. A park of some sort, the area around it dotted with baseball fields and volleyball courts. "Where are we?"

"The suburbs, about fifty miles from my place. I thought you and Sophia could use a little fresh air."

"Is she here?" The thought of letting Sophia toddle around the playground lifted her mood, but the tightness in her chest didn't ease and the throbbing in her head didn't stop.

"She will be soon. I called Serena while you were meeting with Antonio. She's the only one who knows the location of the park. Josh will be with her, but I asked her not to tell him. The fewer people who know where you are, the safer you'll be."

"I...don't know what to say," she admitted. She'd expected to go straight back to his place. She'd thought she'd be spending the next couple of weeks locked inside. Going to the park with Sophia was a gift she couldn't quite believe she was getting.

"You don't have to say anything, but you do have to *do* something," he responded. "Local law enforcement did a sweep of the area. Everything looks good, but while we're here, whatever I say goes. Don't question it, don't doubt it, don't try to do it your own way."

"Okay."

A dark sedan pulled into the space beside theirs, and Annie could see Serena in the driver's seat. She put her hand on the door handle, ready to get her daughter, but Hunter grabbed her wrist.

"That's an easy answer, Annie," he murmured. "A quick one, but it's not going to be so easy to follow through if there's trouble. I want your promise. Whatever happens, you do things my way. Here. At my place. At trial. Wherever and whenever. No more playing maverick. No more trying to go it on your own."

"So, you're bribing me with a trip to the park with my daughter? I promise or I don't get to spend some time outside with Sophia?"

He frowned, his eyes flashing with irritation. "You're getting your time at the park either way, but I want your word because I know it means something for you to give it, and because I don't want to spend the next two weeks worrying that something is going to go down, and you're going to run off half-cocked again."

She could have refused. She knew it. Even if she had, he'd have let go of her wrist, allowed her out of the car. She'd have gotten Sophia and brought her to the swings, and spent a few precious minutes enjoying the sunshine and the cold, crisp air.

But the irritation in his eyes couldn't hide his concern. It couldn't hide the gentle caress of his thumb across the tender skin at the base of her hand. An unconscious gesture, she was sure, but she felt it deep in her soul, where all the dreams she'd built with Joe had lived. It begged those dreams to come to life again.

She couldn't let them, but she could acknowledge that Hunter cared. That no matter what, he wouldn't betray the trust she put in him.

"Okay," she finally said, her throat clogged with emotions she didn't want to feel. "I promise."

He nodded and released his hold.

It seemed as though there should have been more to say, but time was ticking and Sophia was waiting, the cold air and sweet sunshine begging to be enjoyed.

Everything else could be dealt with later.

Right now, all she wanted was a few precious minutes in the park with her daughter.

FIFTEEN

It had been worth it.

That was the conclusion Hunter came to as he watched Annie help Sophia down the slide for what seemed like the twentieth time. Sophia giggled, the sound ringing through the quiet park.

He'd had to pull some strings, ask a few friends from the St. Louis P.D. to help out, but seeing Annie relaxed and happy made it worthwhile.

"I've got to admit, I was a little doubtful when you told me about this," Serena said, her hip resting against the car. She still wore jeans and a fitted T-shirt, her wool coat concealing her firearm. She looked relaxed and natural, but she never stopped scanning the area.

"And now?" he asked, signaling to Josh. Five minutes and they'd have to leave. A half hour wasn't much time, but it was better than being cooped up inside all day.

"It was a good idea. The kid has been fussy all day. I think she just needed some fresh air and sunshine." She shrugged, tucking her hands into the pockets of her coat. "Of course, we all might freeze to death while she's getting it, but it's nice to see her happy. Annie looks happy, too. Dual benefits."

"Exactly."

"You're worried she's going to run before trial, aren't you?"

"I think she'll stick around. I'm just worried that things are getting to her."

"What things?" Serena asked, her gaze tracking a man and his girlfriend who were jogging through the park.

"Being cooped up with a toddler for one. Being cut off from her family and friends for another."

"She knew what she was getting into when she said she'd testify, Hunter. Everything was explained in detail." Like him, Serena played by the rules, and she didn't have a lot of sympathy for the men and women in protective custody.

Do the job. Get them to trial. Move on to the next job.

"That doesn't mean it's been easy for her."

"Maybe Burke is right," she said, suddenly turning her attention to him, her brown eyes looking straight into his.

"About?" He didn't really need to ask.

"You going soft."

"When did he tell you that?"

"Right after you left this morning," she responded

unapologetically. They were a tight-knit group. It went without saying that they would talk about each other, and it went without saying that no one would be offended by that.

"He could be right," Hunter admitted. There was no sense in trying to hide the truth. As long as he played by the book, it didn't matter how he felt about Annie and Sophia.

Serena eyed him for a moment, her gaze steady and maybe a little surprised. "Is this going to affect the case? Do you want to hand it over to someone else?"

"No. On both counts."

"What are you going to do about it?"

"Nothing. I may feel a little differently about this case than I have about others, but I'm going to conduct myself the way I always have."

She nodded, her attention back on the playground and the area surrounding it. She didn't question him further. He hadn't expected that she would. They'd worked together for long enough to build the kind of trust that took a lot to shake.

He glanced at his watch. The half hour that he'd allotted was over, the sun just beginning to slide below the trees. It was time to go. No matter how much he wanted to let Annie and Sophia stay for a while, he wouldn't veer from the plan.

"I'd better get them so we can go back to the safe house," he said.

"I'll warm up the car. They can both ride with me. That'll be easier than moving the car seat."

True, but he would have preferred to have them both in his SUV. Discussing it would waste more time, though. Besides, Serena's plan was a lot more logical than his. As much as he hated to admit it, that was the truth.

Annie and Sophia were still at the slide, Sophia's excited chatter ringing through the quiet evening. There weren't many other people at the park. Early January was too chilly, the air heavy with winter.

Annie looked over her shoulder as he approached, her face bathed in gold from the setting sun.

She smiled. "I guess it's time to go, huh?"

"I'm afraid so." He caught Sophia as she reached the end of the slide, lifting her high into the air and smiling as she giggled.

"Ready to go home, squirt?" he asked.

"Home!" she repeated, but he doubted she really wanted to go back to his guest room. She didn't have much in the way of toys or books there.

"Are you going to take a nap when we get there? Ms. Serena said you didn't sleep at all today," Annie said as she took Sophia from his arms.

"No nap!" Sophia said. "Slide!"

"I wish I could let you stay longer, but a half hour is all we can do." Hunter touched the small of Annie's back, urging her across the playground.

"I'm just thankful we got any time at all," Annie

responded. "It's been months since we've been to the playground. Sophia really enjoyed herself."

"You looked like you were enjoying yourself, too." She still did, her cheeks tinged pink from the cold, her eyes sparkling. Her hair had come out of its ponytail and hung in wild waves to her shoulders. He wanted to smooth the silky strands, let his hands tangle in the soft curls.

"I am. This is the most fun we've had in a while, isn't it, Sophia?" She smiled at her daughter, her expression soft and open. She looked young and sweet, and he thought it would be way too easy to hurt her.

"Once the trial is over, you'll be able to spend a lot more time doing things like this together," he assured her.

"I hope so, but if there's one thing I've learned from Joe's death it's that there are no guarantees. That being the case, I'll just be happy with today." She set Sophia into the car seat and buckled her in, then slid into the seat beside her.

"Everyone set?" Josh asked as he jogged toward them.

Serena opened the driver's door and got in without responding. Hunter wanted to think she hadn't heard, but he thought it was more likely that she'd ignored the question. He'd have to talk to her about it eventually, but they had more pressing things to deal with.

"Yes. We're set," he said, closing Annie's door. "I'll follow you guys back to the house."

"Why don't you ride along with Serena? I can drive your car to your place," Josh suggested, glancing at Serena, a frown pulling at the corners of his mouth. He looked tired, his eyes deeply shadowed.

"Is there a reason why you want me to do that?"

"You're more familiar to Sophia and Annie. It seems like it would be more comfortable for them."

Hunter didn't point out that both were plenty familiar with Josh. He'd just as soon be in the car if something happened, so he pulled out his keys and handed them over. "Don't scratch the paint," he warned.

Josh laughed. "I'll do my best not to, but if there's trouble, I can't make any promises."

"If there's trouble, I don't care what happens to the SUV. Just make sure that all your attention is on keeping Annie and Sophia safe." He rounded the car and slid into the backseat.

"Buckle up," Serena commanded. She didn't comment on Josh's offer or Hunter's acceptance. They were moving forward with the plan, sticking to the program. Just the way they always did.

Serena pulled out of the parking area. Hunter didn't have to look to know that Josh was following. He'd stick close as they made their way back to the house. Burke would be there waiting. Everything was running smoothly, but Hunter couldn't shake the unsettling feeling that trouble was just around the corner.

They drove through a residential area, then merged onto the interstate, heading back to the city. Dusk settled blue-gray over the road, the sun's last golden rays dappling the pavement and the buildings.

A quiet winter evening. If he'd been married, he'd be looking forward to getting home to his family. If he had a nine-to-five job, marriage might have been a possibility.

Sophia grabbed his sleeve.

"Hunt!" she said, her chubby cheeks still pink from the cold. He'd never pictured himself with kids, but if he had, he'd have probably imagined a little girl like Sophia.

"Did you have fun on the slide?" he asked.

"Yes!" she shouted, her high-pitched voice more familiar to him than the voices of his nieces and nephews were. He figured he could pick her out of a crowd blindfolded just by listening to her talk. Being around someone almost constantly would do that to a person.

"You ready to go home and have something to eat?"

"Cookies?" she asked, her eyes the same deep blue as her mother's.

"I don't think your mom is going to let you eat cookies before dinner." He glanced at Annie. She was staring out the window and seemed deep in thought, but he was pretty certain she'd heard his comment.

He'd hoped that going to the park would cheer her up, help her relax a little, but she still seemed tense.

"Annie?" he said, and she met his eyes. Like her daughter, she had cold-tinged cheeks, the pink making her eyes look even bluer. "Sophia wants cookies for dinner."

She touched Sophia's dark curls, her hand trembling slightly. She seemed scared, but he wasn't sure why. She was safer in the car than she'd been at the park. "I don't think so, sweetie. We'll have cookies another night."

"No. Now!" Sophia crowed.

"You can help Mommy cook. We'll make macaroni and…" Annie's voice trailed off and the pink in her cheeks deepened. "Sorry," she said, meeting his eyes. "I'm getting ahead of myself. All that fresh air almost made me forget that we don't have the freedom we used to."

"You'll have it back soon enough," Serena said before Hunter could.

Annie had been reminded of that a few too many times. She kept the thought to herself and looked out the window again. She'd enjoyed every minute of the time they'd spent at the park, and she wasn't going to complain that it was over.

She'd go home, feed Sophia and hopefully put her

to bed early. She needed some time to unwind, to read her Bible, to pray and think about the future. There were so many possibilities opened up to her, so many places she could go. A shiver of excitement raced through her at the thought. As hard as it was to go on without Joe, she would soon have the freedom to make any decision she wanted, to go anywhere she felt led.

That was a heady feeling and a big responsibility.

"You okay?" Hunter murmured, reaching across the car seat and touching her arm.

She had no choice but to look at him, to see the deep dark brown of his eyes, the familiar angle of his jaw. She wanted to touch the stubble there, let her fingers trace the soft curve of his mouth.

"Just thinking about the future. About all the possibilities that are out there," she admitted.

"Getting excited about leaving town?"

"That, too."

"I can have some real-estate brochures brought in. You can look at places in some of the rural towns in the states you said you've wanted to live in," he suggested, and that shiver of excitement shot through her again.

"I'll need a job before I get a house."

"We'll help you work everything out," Serena said, smiling into the rearview mirror. She had an easy manner and a kindness that Annie appreciated. If the circumstances were different, they'd be friends.

"I appreciate it, but after the trial, I want to—"

Hunter's cell phone rang.

"Hold on," he said, taking his phone from his pocket. "Davis here."

He paused, his gaze on Annie.

She couldn't hear the caller, but Hunter's eyes narrowed, his expression suddenly hard and tight. "All right. I'll swing by as soon as we get Annie and Sophia back to the safe house," he finally said.

He shoved the phone back into his pocket.

"What's going on?" Serena asked before Annie could.

"There's been some trouble at Antonio's place."

"What kind of trouble?" Serena frowned.

"An explosive device at his house. His wife saw the package on their front porch. It looked suspicious, so she called him. He called the police."

"And?"

"The bomb squad was called out, and the device was discovered and disarmed without anyone being hurt."

"Thank goodness," Annie murmured.

"Yeah. The package contained low-level explosives. Probably not enough to kill someone."

"Probably? That means it *could* have killed someone," Annie pointed out. "It has to be connected to the explosion yesterday."

"We don't know that," Hunter responded, but from the look on his face, she'd say that he believed it. She'd also say that there was more to the story.

"Something else is going on," she said. "What is it?"

"There was something inside the package with the explosives."

"What?"

"A doll's head."

Serena muttered something under her breath, but Annie was too stunned to speak.

"An evidence team is taking it to the lab for testing, but Burke is on-site, and he says it looks like it's a match for the doll body that was thrown into the safe-house yard."

"Any note with this one?" Serena asked. Obviously, *she* wasn't haven't any trouble speaking.

"No, but if the match is confirmed, I'd say the message was pretty clear."

"It might be clear now, but it would have been difficult to get if the doll head had gotten blown to bits." Serena turned onto Hunter's court. The house was just a few hundred yards in front of the car. For the first time since she'd entered witness protection, Annie couldn't wait to be behind a closed and locked door.

"The evidence team would have found the connection. Whoever left the package was smart enough to know that." Hunter rubbed the back of his neck, his scowl deepening. "He couldn't find Annie, so he made sure to get his point across in another way."

"I think we all knew his point before this." Annie finally managed to speak, her throat dry and thick with fear. "He doesn't want me to testify."

"It doesn't matter what he wants, Annie," Serena said calmly. "We've got you tucked away where he's not going to find you."

"Yet," she mumbled, every thought of a new life in a new place slipping away.

"Ever," Hunter asserted. He reached across the car seat as they pulled into his garage, took her hand, his palm warm and rough against hers. Her heart jumped in response, her pulse racing with a longing she hadn't expected to ever feel again.

She looked into his eyes, saw her surprise and longing reflected in his gaze.

"I'm going to make sure of it," he said, the words soft and gentle, his eyes burning with a promise Annie felt in the depth of her soul.

He meant it, and not just because she was a job that he had to do.

He released her hand and opened his door. "I need to head over to the crime scene. I'll be back as soon as I can."

He got out of the car and hurried to the SUV that was pulling into the garage next to them.

Josh got out. Hunter hopped in.

He was gone before Annie unbuckled Sophia.

"Ready?" Serena asked as she opened Annie's door.

"Sure." She lifted Sophia and got out of the car.

Josh already had the door open, and she walked through the laundry room and into the kitchen. The place was spotless, the high chair set up near the table, a toddler's sippy cup sitting on the tray. Two books were beside it. Both with colorful pictures and different textures on each page. One squeaked as Annie picked it up, and Sophia squealed with delight.

"This will make things a lot easier," Annie said as she buckled Sophia into the seat. "Thank you."

"You can thank Hunter when he gets back. He didn't want us to go back to either safe house again, so he asked Burke to pick up a few things at the store. Hopefully, Burke did okay. He's not big on kids, so I'm not sure he knew what to get."

"The books are great. And the cup." And the fact that Hunter had thought about Sophia and her needs.

"I think he got a few toys, too. They're probably upstairs in your room. Go ahead and get what you want for dinner. I have some work to do." She walked out of the kitchen as Josh walked in from the laundry room.

He watched Serena's retreating figure then turned to Annie. "I'm going to watch the monitors. You go ahead and do whatever you need to."

He settled into a chair at the table, his focus on the computer monitor.

There were a lot of questions Annie wanted to ask. Most of them about the doll head that was being examined at the crime lab. She knew Josh wouldn't have any answers.

The best thing she could do was keep busy, keep focused on Sophia and on keeping her happy, healthy and safe until the trial.

It seemed as though it should be easy enough, but even as she dragged out pans and pots and ingredients and began cooking a dinner that could feed six, she couldn't stop thinking about the doll, about the men who'd taken it and the man who was using it as a threat.

She understood what was at stake for the crime syndicate that Saunders and Fiske worked for, but it seemed almost inconceivable that the men that Hunter often referred to as low-level thugs could be so important that the people they worked for would kill to keep them from going to jail.

She sighed, whisking flour and melted butter together in a pot while Sophia played with the books.

God was in control.

That was the one thing she knew for sure.

And it was the only thing that mattered.

He would get her through this the same way He'd brought her through everything else. When it was over, she'd be stronger because of it, more confident, more ready to raise her daughter alone.

Too bad the thought didn't excite her.

Too bad she'd much rather be raising Sophia with someone else.

An image of Hunter flashed through her mind, his long tan fingers touching Sophia's curls. He had a tenderness to him that she never would have imagined was hidden beneath his gruff exterior. Once she'd seen it, she couldn't deny that it was there.

She couldn't deny what it did to her heart, either.

A heart that was going to end up broken again if she wasn't careful.

The problem was, she didn't want to be careful.

She wanted to be carefree and young and completely convinced that everything would work out just fine.

Time had changed her. Circumstances had changed her. She didn't regret those changes, but there were plenty of times when she wished that she could just…be. Without worrying, without wondering, without doubting herself and her feelings.

Maybe one day she'd get back to that.

But she really didn't think it would be anytime soon.

SIXTEEN

It was nearly midnight when Hunter returned to the house. He'd stayed at the crime scene until all the evidence had been collected, and then he'd followed the technicians back to the lab.

Fortunately, two of the techs were friends, and they'd agreed to compare the doll body and head while he was there. It had been obvious to everyone that the two were a match. Same materials for head and body. Cut marks on each had been consistent. Someone had used scissors to behead the doll. There was no obvious DNA evidence. The techs had still been looking when Hunter drove back home.

The lights were off as he pulled into the driveway. He parked there instead of the garage, knowing that Burke was probably inside watching the monitors.

The cul-de-sac was quiet, the full moon casting long shadows across yards and houses. Nothing moved as he walked to the front door and unlocked it. So far, the plan was working. With only the four-member team privy to Annie and Sophia's whereabouts, they'd maintained the integrity of the safe house.

Burke had been right. Skirting protocol for a change had benefited everyone. After years of living by the rules, Hunter still wasn't sure how he felt about that.

The front door opened before he reached it, Burke hovering in the threshold.

"How'd it go?" he asked before Hunter even stepped into the house.

"About like we expected it would. The doll body and head were a perfect match. No physical evidence that might yield DNA. The evidence team is still looking, but it's not likely they'll find it." He shrugged out of his coat as he stepped past Burke.

The house smelled...different.

He inhaled, his stomach jumping to attention as he realized why. Food. Not fast food. Not ramen noodles. Real food. The kind he only ate when he got together with family.

"Man, that smells good!" he murmured.

"It tasted good, too. Homemade mac and cheese. Oven-fried chicken. Caesar salad. That woman sure can cook." Burke grinned. "Wish we'd known that a month ago. We could have had her making meals every night."

"You're talking about Annie?"

"Who else?"

"It's not her job to cook for anyone but herself

and her child, Burke. I hope you didn't ask to join them for their meal." He kept his tone neutral, but he wasn't pleased. He was man enough to admit it was because he wanted to be the one who'd sat down and enjoyed a meal with Annie and Sophia.

"No need to jump to her defense, Hunt. I was minding my own business, trying to ignore all the great smells that were coming from the kitchen, and she invited me. What kind of man would I be if I said no?"

"One who was doing his job?"

"It's not my job to turn down a good meal," Burke insisted. "And let me tell you something. It was the best twenty minutes on the job that I've had in years."

"That good, huh?"

"Better than good. It was like eating Mom's home cooking. If Mom had been able to cook."

Hunter laughed. "Well, don't rub my nose in it. I ate a package of cheese crackers four hours ago, and that's all I've had since this afternoon. Any trouble while I was gone?"

"None. It's been quiet inside and outside."

Floorboards creaked above their heads, and Burke looked up at the ceiling. "Until now. Annie probably wants an update. She hounded me about it until Sophia went to bed."

"Hounding? That doesn't sound like Annie."

"Asking? Beseeching? Begging for information? Pick your poison."

"I thought you liked Annie," Hunter responded mildly.

"I did, and I do. After the meal I just ate, I'd even be tempted to follow her to whatever town she's going to next, but you probably have a lot more staying power than I do, and I'd hate to hurt her. She's already been hurt enough, right?"

"Right," Hunter agreed.

"So, I'm leaving her to you. Of course, if *you* end up hurting her, I'll have to take you out back and beat some sense into you."

"You're making a lot of assumptions there, Burke."

"Observations. Not assumptions. I've worked with you for almost ten years. I know how you operate, and I know this case is different. You may be putting on your professional pants and doing the job the way you always do, but it's different. Are you going to tell me it's not?"

"No."

"Good. Then we're on the same page."

"What page would that be?"

"The one where I tell you to be careful, and you tell me to mind my own business."

"I'll skip my part in it. This *is* your business. Until we get the Delacortes to trial."

"Then what?" Burke asked.

"Then it's my business." And he wasn't quite sure

what he had planned. Just let Annie and Sophia go to their new home and their new lives? Eventually, he'd forget about them. He'd continue on the way he'd been going, pouring every ounce of his energy into his job.

Was it enough?

That was the question that haunted him.

The loose board at the top of the stairs creaked, and he knew Annie was on her way down.

"I'd better go check the monitor," Burke said, slipping from the room as footsteps sounded in the stairway. Seconds later, Annie appeared, her hair loose and wild with untamed curls. She'd changed into pink sweatpants and a white T-shirt. The pants hung low on her hips, the T-shirt just skimming their waistband. She smiled when she saw him, and his heart responded.

"You're back," she said, dropping onto the sofa and pulling her knees up to her chest. Her arms were thin and well muscled, her fingers long and narrow. Pretty hands. Pretty arms. Beautiful woman.

"And you're awake." He sat beside her, inhaling the fresh clean scent of shampoo and soap.

"I wanted to hear what you found out, so I stayed up."

"The doll body and head are a match," he told her without preamble. There was no sense beating around the bush.

"That's not a surprise." She rubbed the back of

her neck and sighed. "Was there anything else? Any evidence that will help you find the person who planted the bomb?"

"The evidence team is still looking. If there's something to be found, they should know it in the next day or two."

"I guess that's it, then. More waiting." She dropped her chin to her knees, her hair spilling over her arms. He wanted to put an arm around her shoulders, tell her everything was going to be okay.

There was an invisible wall between them, though. One made of his commitment to the marshals.

"The waiting won't be so bad," he assured her, touching her arm, the warmth of her skin shooting through him. He leaned in, unconsciously moving closer. "I'm having the real-estate brochures that I promised you shipped to my office. They should be here in a couple of days."

"Great." She sounded so pitiful that he chuckled, tucking a strand of her hair behind her ear so that he could see her face.

"The time will go quickly. I promise."

"That's the second promise you've made to me in twenty-four hours. Maybe you should quit while you're ahead."

"Quit what?"

"Making promises." She met his eyes, her raven-black eyebrows drawn together, her cheeks smooth and pale. "They can be awfully difficult to keep."

"Not if the person giving them takes them seriously."

"I guess you're right. Like you said earlier, I can't judge everyone on…"

"One person's failures?"

"Something like that." She smiled wearily, her eyes so darkly shadowed the skin looked bruised.

"You need to get some sleep, Annie."

"So do you, but we're both wide-awake. Did you eat dinner?"

"Not yet."

"I put a plate of food in the fridge for you, if you're hungry. Want me to heat it up for you?"

She turned toward the kitchen, but he snagged her waist. "What I want," he murmured, "isn't something that I can have right now."

Her eyes widened, but she didn't pull away.

"You're a beautiful woman, Annie. I'd have to be a fool not to notice."

She laughed nervously, slipping from his grasp and taking a few steps away. "Beautiful? I'm wearing sweats and a T-shirt and my hair hasn't been combed since sometime this morning."

"It's not clothes or hair that make you beautiful. It's the way you treat your daughter. The way you treat everyone in your life. Your faith. Your positive attitude." He didn't hold back, didn't try to pretend anything different than what was. They both deserved the truth, and they both had to decide what to do with it.

"Hunter..." She ran a hand over her hair, shifted from foot to foot.

"What?"

She shrugged. "I don't want to be lied to again. I don't want to play the fool. I don't want to think I'm going to have everything and then find out that I've got nothing."

"So, you'd rather spend the rest of your life alone?"

"I thought I would. Now I'm not so sure."

"Just like with everything else in your life right now, you have some time to think about it."

She shook her head and smiled. "True. Too much time, if you ask me."

"I can think of a way to distract you. For tonight anyway."

Her eyes widened; her mouth dropped open. "What?"

"Come here." He led her across the room and opened a cabinet in the bookcase. His uncle sent him photos of the ranch several times a year. Probably in an attempt to entice Hunter back to Montana. Hunter hadn't had the heart to throw any of them out. He pulled out a shoe box. "Take a look."

She opened the lid, lifted a photo of a ranch house, its white clapboard siding gleaming in the afternoon sun. In the distance, white-tipped mountains stretched toward the sky. "It's beautiful. Where was it taken?"

"My uncle's ranch in Montana."

"Wow!" She lifted another picture. This one of a cow and her calf. "This is the kind of place I wanted to live when I was a kid."

"Did you grow out of wanting it?"

"I married a man who liked the city." She smiled as she studied a photo of Hunter's uncle Samuel. Tall and narrow, his face deeply tanned, he wore a cowboy hat, scuffed boots and a layer of dust from hours spent working cattle. "Who is this?"

"My uncle."

"Your father's brother?"

"My mother's."

"Do you visit him every year?"

"I haven't been back in a long time, but Uncle Samuel sends me pictures every year. I think he'd like me to come back."

"Why haven't you?"

"Work keeps me busy."

She set the photos back in the box, looked straight into his eyes. "Work should never be more important than family."

He knew that, but he'd forgotten it for a while.

He frowned, taking the photo of his uncle from the box. He'd aged, his dark hair liberally salted with gray, the lines on his face deeper than they'd been. "You're right, Annie. I need to make time to see Sam."

"I'm glad we agree. Now, how about you go eat the food I left for you?" Annie held the box out toward Hunter, but he shook his head.

"Take them upstairs and look through them. Maybe you'll decide Montana is the place to settle."

"If the rest of the photos are like the first three, I'm going to be more than a little tempted to do just that." The house, the cattle, the weather-worn cowboy—they appealed to Annie at a visceral level. Made her think of home and family and long nights spent next to warm fires.

"If you like the look of Montana, I can start searching around. We should be able to find you a nice little property and a job," Hunter offered. He looked as rugged as his uncle, his jaw dark with a five-o'clock shadow, his hair slightly ruffled.

She could imagine him standing just where his uncle had been, cowboy boots and hat, dust-covered jeans. He would make a perfect rancher. She could imagine being there with him, her arm wrapped around his waist, her hands resting on his firm side.

She pulled her thoughts up short, glancing away from Hunter's dark eyes. "I...don't know."

"That's fine. I'm not asking you to make a decision now. I'm just offering you the option."

"Okay," she said. "I'll look through the pictures, and I'll think about Montana."

"Good." Hunter sounded legitimately pleased, his smile as warm and welcome as summer sunshine.

If he'd opened his arms right then, she would have walked straight into them. No regrets. No second thoughts. She would have laid her head against his chest, listened to the solid thud of his heart.

He didn't.

She didn't.

But she was pretty sure they both wanted to.

"I'd better go upstairs," she murmured, afraid if she didn't leave, she'd do exactly what she shouldn't and throw herself into his arms.

"Good night, Annie."

The new name sounded wonderfully familiar coming from his lips.

Her heart thumped in response, her pulse racing with feelings she'd thought she would never have again.

She clutched the box to her chest, ran upstairs and closed herself in the room with Sophia.

SEVENTEEN

Twenty days.

Nearly three weeks.

That was how long Annie had been locked in Hunter's house. Aside from appearing in court, she hadn't been anywhere else, done anything else.

Now it was nearly over.

Not just those twenty days, but the year she'd spent in witness protection.

Annie wasn't quite sure how she felt about that. Relieved? Excited? Scared? A little of the first two and a lot of the last.

Today had been the last day of the trial. The jury was already deliberating. She'd done everything she could to make sure Fiske and Saunders paid for what they'd done to Joe. She hoped it had been enough. Prayed it had been.

One way or another, tomorrow would be the first day of the rest of her life.

It felt strange to think of living without rules and protocol, bizarre to think that she could wake up every morning and go through her day without fear and anxiety.

Even stranger to think she'd be living in a house alone with Sophia. No armed guards checking in on them. No security cameras or computer monitors.

No Hunter.

Her stomach sank, something like sorrow clawing up her throat and lodging there.

"Stop it! You've been waiting for this day for over a year. You're happy. Not sad," she muttered.

She didn't quite believe herself.

She glanced in the dresser mirror, smoothing the collar of her dress. A soft dove-gray, it had a 1950s vibe, the Peter Pan collar and slim pencil skirt demure enough for court and fashionable enough to appeal to both the men and women on the jury.

At least, that was what Steven had said when he'd handed it to her. She'd worn it on the first day of trial, and he'd told her to keep it. She had to admit, it looked good paired with black pumps and a neat chignon. She applied mascara, blush, lip gloss—the same way she'd done every day before trial for the past week. Tonight, she was doing it for a different reason.

She was going to see her parents for the first time in over a year. Just thinking about it made her pulse race with happiness. They hadn't approved of her testifying. They certainly hadn't wanted her in protective custody. They'd always loved her, though.

They'd been her biggest support system in the weeks following Joe's death, and it was going to be really good to spend time with them.

"Pretty, Mommy!" Sophia said, tugging at Annie's hem.

"Thank you, sweetie." She lifted her, inhaling the sweet powdery scent of baby shampoo. She wanted so much for her daughter, and she was going to work hard to provide those things. Not a big house or fancy cars or anything material. Just love and security, faith and happiness.

Tomorrow.

The first day of forever, and it felt bittersweet because of Hunter.

"Guess what we're doing tonight, Sophia?" she asked, setting her wiggling daughter back on the floor and doing her best to ignore the fact that moving on with her life meant leaving Hunter behind.

"We're going to see Grandma and Grandpa," she continued as Sophia danced around the room. "Doesn't that sound like fun?"

"Yay!" Sophia clapped her hands, but Annie didn't think she had any idea what that meant. The last time she'd seen her grandparents, she'd been just a year old.

"We're going to meet them, and Hunter is going to take us all to dinner." They were going to a small restaurant on the outskirts of St. Louis. A long drive, but Hunter didn't want to take any chances.

"Cookies?" Sophia wanted to know.

"No cookies," Annie said with a laugh.

"Yes cookies!" Sophia responded with an impish grin.

"You know what you are? You're a cookie monster!" Annie said, tickling Sophia's belly and then smoothing down the front of her velvet dress. Royal blue with a wide sash and a crinoline underskirt, it was the perfect complement for Sophia's dark hair and fair skin.

Hunter had chosen well.

But then, Hunter seemed to always do the right thing and make the right choices. The way he'd treated Annie was the perfect example. He'd made no secret of the fact that he found her attractive. Since the night he'd let her look at photos of his uncle's ranch, he'd been even more solicitous, more caring. He'd talked to her late into the night, listened to her worries about the trial and about her life after it. They'd sat in church together, arm pressed against arm, talked about the sermons afterward. They'd shared a thousand moments together, but Hunter had been professional through it all. He'd never crossed the line, never tried to go after more than quiet conversation and easy companionship.

There had been a few times when *she'd* wanted to, though.

"I'm not cookie monster," Sophia squealed happily.

"You are." Annie chuckled, but her stomach felt hollow, her heart empty.

Someone knocked on the door, and she opened it, knowing Hunter would be on the other side.

He'd changed into dark slacks and a blue dress shirt, his hair brushing his collar. He looked good. Better than good. He looked like a man she'd like to have dinner with, a guy she'd love to spend an afternoon walking through the park with. He looked like what forever might have been if she hadn't met and married Joe.

"Looks like you're ready to go," he said, stepping into the room.

"We've been ready for a half hour. I guess I'm a little anxious." She brushed a hand down her skirt, smoothing out invisible wrinkles.

"I'm sure your parents are, too. We'll leave in ten minutes. Just like we planned."

"The trial is over. I thought we could loosen up a little. Maybe leave in nine minutes instead of ten."

He laughed, scooping Sophia into his arms when she tugged on his pant leg. "Sounds like you're really wanting to live on the wild side, Annie."

"Not wild, just…freer."

"Tomorrow will be here before you know it, and I have some news that will probably make your new life a lot easier."

"What?"

"Antonio just called me."

Her heart jumped at the words. The attorneys had given their closing arguments that morning, and the jury had been deliberating since then. She'd been praying for a quick decision. She'd be leaving town the next day, one way or another, but she wanted to leave knowing that both men were going to be behind bars. "What did he say?"

"The jury has finished deliberation. The verdict was unanimous. Saunders was convicted on the second-degree-murder charge. Fiske was convicted of being an accessory. Both of them are going to jail. Saunders will probably spend the rest of his life there."

"How about Fiske?"

"Hopefully, he'll be there for a good long time. He wasn't the trigger man, though, and it's hard to prove that he knew Saunders was going to pull the trigger." He touched her shoulder, his hand sliding to her nape. His palm was warm and rough, his fingers slipping beneath her collar.

"It's over, Annie. Your life is yours again. All you have to do is decide what to do with it," he murmured.

"That seemed so much easier a couple of weeks ago. Now that it's here, and I'm ready to start over, I'm not sure I know what I want."

"A pretty little house on a couple of acres of land. A nice job at a nursery school where you can bring Sophia. A chance to go back to college and become an elementary schoolteacher so that you and Sophia will be on the same schedule when she's older."

"You've been listening," she said, her pulse thrumming.

"Always." He tugged her closer, their bodies just centimeters apart. "Have you thought any more about going to Montana? Because I've done the research and found a nice little town a few hundred miles from my uncle's place. There's a rental there. It's on acreage with farms all around."

"That's funny because, last night, I dreamed that I was living in a farmhouse and that there were cattle grazing in a field behind it." In the dream, she'd been sitting on a porch swing with Sophia, and Hunter had been walking toward them. It had been the best dream she'd had in months, and she hadn't wanted to wake up because she hadn't wanted it to end.

"What if I said that the owner of the property is willing to rent it out beginning tomorrow?"

"I'd say I was tempted." Really tempted.

"What if I told you that there was an opening for a teacher at the local nursery school in that town, and what if I told you that they'd be thrilled to have you teach there?"

"I'd say that you work fast."

"I've been looking since the night we talked about my uncle's ranch. I found the nursery school first, then hunted for the property. One of the teachers at the school is going on maternity leave. You could step in for her as a long-term sub. She'll be out for a year."

"By the time she returns, I'd be settled into the community and would have some connections with the people who live there. I could probably find another job pretty easily," she said as much to herself as to him.

"Does that mean you like the idea?" he asked, smiling into her eyes.

"I love the idea."

"I'm glad. I always said that if I left St. Louis, Montana is where I'd want to be." He set Sophia down.

"What does that have to do with anything?" she asked, but she knew. She could see it in his eyes.

"Today, I'm still the marshal assigned to protect you. Tomorrow, I'll just be a man who wants to spend a little more time with you. If that's not okay with you, tell me now."

There were plenty of reasons why she should.

She'd been through too much because of Joe. She didn't want to risk her heart again. She was perfectly capable of living her life without a man in it.

She could sit down and write reason after reason, but none of them meant anything when she was looking into Hunter's eyes. "I think it is."

"Think?" he murmured. "I'd rather you know, because I do."

"I—"

"Hunt? You up there?" Burke called from the bottom of the stairs.

"Yeah." Hunter walked to the doorway, his gaze still on Annie. He wanted an answer, and he deserved one.

Finally, he broke eye contact and looked out into the hall. "What's up, Burke?"

"Just got a call from the St. Louis P.D. Fiske wants to talk to you."

"About?"

"He says he knows who's responsible for the bombs and the threats against Annie."

"And he's just coming forward now? That information would have been more useful to him before the trial." And the fact that he was willing to reveal it now put Hunter's guard up.

He stepped into the hall, met Burke at the top of the stairs.

"He said he didn't have the information until a few days ago, and he was trying to decide how he wanted to use it."

"That sounds like Fiske. Always looking for the next deal." The guy had a rap sheet filled with petty crime and illegal deals. He knew how to manipulate the system, and Hunter had a feeling that was exactly what he was trying to do.

"He's hoping the judge will give him a lighter sentence if he cooperates with us on this," Burke said. "At least, that's what he told the lieutenant who just called the office. Serena passed the information on to me."

"I'm surprised she didn't pass it to me."

"Your shift ended three minutes ago." Burke crossed his arms over his chest, looked past Hunter. "You look gorgeous tonight, Annie," he said without missing a beat, his flirtatious smile working its way under Hunter's skin.

"Thank you." Annie stepped up beside Hunter, a subtle flowery perfume drifting in the air as she moved. His muscles tightened with longing, every cell in his body responding to her. He didn't reach for her, but he wanted to.

Annie wasn't the only one who'd been itching for more freedom. He wanted it, too, with a desperation that surprised him.

"What's going on?" she asked, her gaze jumping from Burke to Hunter.

"Fiske says he has information about the person who's been threatening you," he responded. "He wants to give it to me."

"Tonight?" She frowned, her dark eyebrows pulling together.

"Sentencing is tomorrow, and he's hoping that the judge will give him a break if he helps us out," Burke offered.

"I don't think he deserves a break," Annie said, her eyes flashing with indignation.

"You're right, but if it means getting another criminal off the street, I'm willing to listen to what he has to say."

"Glad to hear it," Burke said. "Want me to call St. Louis P.D. and let them know you're on the way?"

"Sure."

"But…" Annie's voice trailed off, and she shook her head. "I guess this is more important than dinner with my family."

"There's no reason for you to miss out on that," Burke cut in before Hunter could respond. "I'm on duty anyway. I can bring you."

Not a good idea.

That was what Hunter wanted to say, but there was no reason for Annie to skip dinner. He'd arranged everything, made sure only a few people knew the plan. She'd be safe as long as Burke was with her. "What do you think, Hunter?" Burke prodded. "You want me to go ahead with the dinner plan?"

Hunter met Annie's eyes. She wouldn't complain if he said no, but he'd made a promise. The only way he'd break it was if he thought that keeping it would put her in danger.

So far, his team had been able to keep her whereabouts secret. Though the computer forensic team had come up empty in its search for the marshals' information leak, there hadn't been any further breach of confidence. There was no reason to believe that things had changed.

He still wanted to be with her when she visited her family.

He met Burke's eyes. He probably knew exactly what Hunter was thinking.

"That should work," he said, but he wasn't all that thrilled about it. "Just make sure you stick around while she and her parents are eating dinner. They'll be out in public and—"

"I've been doing this job for a long time, Hunter. I think I know how it works," Burke said drily. "Besides, the likelihood that we'll run into any trouble is slim to none. The trial is over. Whoever was threatening Annie has nothing to gain from continuing."

"You're probably right, but I like to err on the side of caution."

"I think you know me well enough to know that I feel the same," Burke responded, smiling in Annie's direction.

She looked tense, her expression tight and closed.

Whatever she was thinking, she kept silent, snagging Sophia as she tried to toddle past.

"If it's going to be a problem," she murmured, "we can skip the visit."

"No problem at all," Burke said cheerfully. "It looks like you and Sophia are ready, so I'll run and get cleaned up, and then we can take off."

He jogged down the stairs, probably heading to his room.

"You okay with this?" Hunter asked, pressing his hand to Annie's back and urging her down the stairs.

"Why wouldn't I be?"

"I don't know, but you seem tense."

"I guess I'm just used to having you drive me everywhere. It will seem strange to have someone else doing it."

"If you want me to put off the meeting with Fiske—"

"That would be a ridiculous thing for me to ask you to do." She cut him off.

"But if you asked, I'd do it." He handed her Sophia's coat, then took hers from the closet.

"I know," she sighed as he helped her into the coat. "That's what makes you so hard to resist."

"Who says you have to resist me?" He pulled her coat collar up around her neck, his fingers sliding against cool skin.

"Common sense. I don't want to let myself believe in something that isn't possible."

"Anything is possible, Annie. Even us spending time together after you leave St. Louis."

"At what cost? You giving up everything you love, everything you've worked for for me?"

"If that's what I decided to do, would it be such a bad thing?" He wanted to know. He *needed* to know, because he'd been thinking about it a lot, wondering if he could let Annie and Sophia walk away and not spend the rest of his life regretting it.

She shook her head. "You're not thinking clearly. You're letting momentary feelings interfere with your long-term goals."

"You don't know what my goals are." *He* didn't know what they were. Not anymore.

"No, but I know this. I gave up everything for Joe. All the dreams about having a house in the country and a white picket fence and going back to college—I let go of those things because it wasn't what Joe wanted. I don't ever want to do that to someone else. I'm not going to let—"

Burke walked into the room, cutting off whatever she planned to say.

"All right," he said, his gaze jumping from Hunter to Annie and back again. If he sensed their tension, he didn't comment on it. "I'm ready."

"Great," Annie responded, turning her back to Hunter, her shoulders stiff. "Let's get out of here."

She headed for the laundry room, but Burke grabbed her hand, the gesture a little too familiar for Hunter's liking. "Give me two minutes to switch the car seat, then come out to the garage."

"I can help," Annie insisted, but Burke shook his head. He was following protocol, doing what he was supposed to do. Hopefully, he'd keep that up for the rest of the night.

"All right." Annie glanced at her watch, at the wall, at the door to the laundry room. She looked at just about everything but Hunter as Burke walked away.

"You can't avoid looking at me forever," Hunter pointed out.

"I can try." She offered a wry smile and finally met his eyes. "I don't want you to make a mistake, Hunter. I don't want you to give up something perfectly good for something that might be—"

"Even better?"

"That's not what I was going to say."

"But it's how I see things. If I decide to follow you into witness protection—"

"I told you, I can't let you do that!"

"*If* I do, it'll be because I think that what I'll have with you and Sophia is better than what I've found in my job."

"But—"

"Nothing needs to be decided right now." He cut her off, because discussing it wouldn't change the way he felt. He'd already requested a few weeks of personal leave, because he needed time to clear his head, think things through. "It doesn't even need to be decided tomorrow. So, how about you just go enjoy dinner with your parents, and we'll talk about it later?"

"Later, I'll be in Montana," she reminded him

with a sad smile, "starting my new life, and you'll be here living your life. Before either of us knows it, we'll have moved on and forgotten each other."

"In that case…" he said, snagging her wrist and tugging her closer.

Burke had been right. Hunter's shift was over. He'd completed the job, had gotten Annie to trial, made sure she'd testified, done all of it by the book.

Now he was done playing by the rules, finished being the marshal protecting a witness.

"…I'd better give both of us something to remember."

"What?" Her eyes widened, but she didn't back away.

"This," he murmured, his lips brushing hers.

Her muscles tensed, then relaxed, her body leaning into his, her free arm wrapping around his waist.

She pulled him closer, their lips touching again, their breath mingling.

Every thought fled, every worry gone. All that mattered was that moment and that kiss.

"Annie!" Burke called. "You coming?"

Annie broke away, her cheeks pink, her breath heaving.

Hunter wanted nothing more than to pull her back into his arms again.

"Annie?" Burke's footsteps sounded on the kitchen floor.

"Coming!" Annie said, her voice shaky, her eyes filled with the same longing Hunter felt. "Good night."

Then she turned on her heels and ran from the room.

EIGHTEEN

He'd kissed her.

She'd kissed him!

Annie couldn't stop thinking about it. Not as she buckled Sophia into her car seat or got into the car beside her. Not as Burke pulled out of the garage or drove through the quiet neighborhood.

They'd be meeting her parents soon. For the first time in a year, Annie would get the chance to hug her mother and father, talk to them, tell them how much she'd missed them. That should be all she was thinking about, but she could still feel the heat of Hunter's lips, still feel the warmth of his hand against her waist.

"You excited about seeing your folks?" Burke asked, glancing into the rearview mirror and meeting her eyes.

Thank goodness the sun had set an hour ago, and her pink cheeks were hidden by darkness. "Yes. Where are we meeting them?"

The words sounded shaky to her, but Burke didn't seem to notice.

"At the house of a retired marshal. Bud Hollingsworth. You've met him, right?"

"I'm not sure."

"Doesn't matter if you haven't. We're just going to park outside his place and pick your folks up.

"Hunter allotted two hours at the restaurant. After that, I'm supposed to take you back to our place so you can pack up and get ready for tomorrow."

He didn't seem to be asking questions about the plan, but she nodded anyway. "That's right."

"It's a reasonable plan, but I'm not sure that we have to follow the schedule exactly. You'd like to spend a little more time with your parents, right?"

"It would be nice, but we should probably just stick to Hunter's plan." She was already packed, the one suitcase that she'd brought to Milwaukee when she'd left town and then carried with her when she'd returned stuffed full of the things she'd be taking to her new home.

In Montana?

She'd loved the idea from the moment she'd seen photos of the state, but she wasn't sure how she felt about it now that Hunter was talking about leaving the marshals.

For her.

"You and Hunter seem to get along well," Burke

said casually, but she didn't think there was anything casual about the comment.

"I get along well with everyone on the team."

"True, but after tomorrow, you're not going to spend much time thinking about any of us." He turned onto Steven's street. "I'm sure you will spend a lot of time thinking about Hunter."

"And?" She wasn't going to deny it, but she wasn't going to have a long conversation about it, either.

"Nothing. I just wanted to make sure you and Hunter are on the same page. I might like to give him a hard time, but we've been friends for years. I don't want to see him make a big mistake."

"You think I would be a mistake?"

"I think that leaving what is certain for something that isn't could be a big mistake, but I've always been a risk taker, and I'd be lying if I said I wasn't enjoying seeing Hunter turn into one."

"I wish he weren't."

"Why?" Burke pulled up to the curb in front of a beautiful two-story house and turned to face her. "The best things life has to offer can't be found in an office or at a job. If Hunter has finally figured that out, who are either of us to try to tell him differently. And that," he said, opening his door, "is the end of my free advice session. You want any more, you have to pay."

"Thanks." She laughed.

"Don't mention it. Now, stay put while I come around. Hunter will have my head if I don't follow protocol."

He got out and shut the door. Darkness pressed against the car windows, but lights shone from the house where Annie's parents waited. Annie was pretty sure that she saw her father peering out from behind the closed front curtains. "We're here," she said to Sophia as she lifted her from the car seat.

Burke opened her door, cold air bathing her cheeks and spearing through her coat.

"Okay. We're going straight to the front door," Burke said, his voice tight.

"Is something wrong?"

"I don't think so."

"I don't think I like that you're not one hundred percent sure."

She got out of the car. The front door was only a few hundred feet away, her parents waiting just beyond it. She wanted to run to the front stoop, open the door and throw herself into her parents' arms.

"Come on." Burke glanced at the lot across the street. It looked dark and foreboding, the trees that edged the property clumped close together, their shadows stretching across pavement lit by streetlights.

She took a step away from the car and a gunshot split the night, the sound shattering the winter silence.

"Get down!" Burke shouted, knocking her forward as another gunshot exploded. She fell to her knees, just barely managing to keep Sophia in her arms.

"Stay down," he muttered, pulling his gun from its holster, something wet and dark spreading across his shoulder.

Blood!

"You've been shot!" she cried.

"It's not serious. Just a flesh wound, and I deserved it for making a rookie mistake. I should have parked in the driveway close to the door," he growled. "We've got to find better cover than this car. I'll distract him. You try to get around the side of the house. Stay down, though. Do you understand?"

"Yes." But she was terrified, her heart beating so loudly that she could barely hear Sophia's soft cries.

"It's okay," she murmured to her daughter, holding her close as Burke straightened, firing several gunshots in a row.

She crawled toward the thick shrubs, freezing when gunfire erupted from the trees across the street.

Burke grunted and fell back, lying still on the ground.

She darted toward him, realized her mistake a moment too late.

A dark shadow sprinted around the side of the

car and snagged her arm, a tall hulking figure dragging her farther from safety. Black ski mask. Black gloves. Glittering eyes that she could just see peering out from the knit mask.

Cold metal pressed against her forehead, the pressure so hard, tears burned in her eyes.

"You fight me and the kid dies. You hear what I'm saying?" her attacker hissed.

She nodded because she couldn't get any words past the fear in her throat.

The front door of Hollingsworth's house flew open, and her father appeared. He was older than she remembered, his lined face clearly visible in the outdoor light.

"Let her go!" he shouted, stepping out onto the front stoop. "We've already called the cops. They'll be here any minute."

"Go back inside, old man." Her attacker raised his gun, aimed.

"No!" Annie knocked his arm and the bullet shattered the light above her father's head. The lights inside the house went off as well, the entire yard going dark.

"Dad!" she shouted, dodging toward the house and nearly falling backward as her attacker grabbed her collar.

"Shut up! Get in the car," he growled, shoving her into Burke's car, snagging keys that had fallen from Burke's hand. "One more stunt like that, and I will kill your daughter. You'll get to watch her die. Would you like that?"

He pressed in beside her, forcing her into the passenger seat as he got behind the wheel.

Annie thought she heard sirens as he slammed the door, but her heart was pounding so loudly in her ears that she couldn't be sure.

She had to stall, get him to hesitate long enough for the police to arrive.

"I need to put Sophia in the car seat," she said, speaking through the cotton that seemed to have filled her mouth and throat.

"And I need to get you somewhere where no one will find you," he snapped. "So, I guess you better hold on tight to the kid."

He stepped on the gas, and the car jumped forward, Sophia nearly slamming into the dashboard, her cries escalating.

"And get that brat to shut up! Do you hear me?" the man shouted.

Annie's hands shook as she pulled Sophia closer, singing quietly in her ear as she buckled the seat belt around both of them. It wouldn't help if they were in a crash, but it made her feel better. More in control.

She needed to think, not panic. Needed to come up with a plan that would get her out of the car and give her a chance to escape. Or, at least, to find a way to save Sophia.

Please, God, help me save her. Please, let me get her out of this alive, she prayed silently.

Her kidnapper turned down a side street, flying through the residential area and speeding downtown. She didn't know this section of St. Louis, and it didn't look like a part of town that she wanted to know.

Tall brick buildings pressed close together, most of them boarded up. Graffiti offered the only splashes of color in the gray-black world.

"Where are you taking us?"

"Somewhere where we can have a little chat."

"About what?"

He turned down a narrow alley between two huge buildings. Both looked abandoned, windows broken and doors boarded over.

"My brother, and what you did to him," he said, parking the car and grabbing her arm. "We're getting out my side, and we're going into the building. Don't bother screaming. There's no one around to hear."

He dragged her from the vehicle, nearly breaking her hold on Sophia. Annie tightened her grip, fear beating a hard, hollow rhythm in her chest.

"Move!" He pressed a gun to her side, forcing her across a crumbling sidewalk. Three steps led down to a basement entrance and the only door in the building that wasn't covered with slabs of plywood.

He yanked the door open and pushed her into the dark dank interior. It smelled like mold and death.

She gagged, trying to see in the pitch-black darkness.

"Now," her attacker said, flicking on a light that barely illuminated the area around them. Old factory equipment and machines littered the area, blocking her view of anything beyond the place where they stood.

"Let's get started." He pulled off his ski mask, his thick brown hair standing up, his eyes dark like deep pools of malice. The face looked familiar. She'd looked into eyes like this before. Seen the same malice and hatred in them. He wasn't Saunders, but he could almost have been his twin.

"You're Saunders's brother," she gasped, taking a step back.

"That's right." He pulled a cell phone from his pocket, the gun lax in his left hand as he dialed. "Hey, boss. It's me. I got them. Yep." He grinned, his gaze never leaving Annie. "The kid's with her. It went down pretty easy. Not sure if I killed the marshal, though. What do you want me to do now?"

Annie took another step back as he listened to the answer.

Please, God. Please.

Her heart thundered as she scanned the room, the darkness beyond the one bare bulb so complete that she couldn't make out an avenue of escape.

Sophia whimpered, and she patted her back.

"It's okay, sweetie. Everything is okay."

Sophia stuck her thumb in her mouth and lay her head against Annie's shoulder, trusting that the words were true.

"Don't worry," Saunders's brother finally said. "She's not going to say a word to anyone about anything. Are you?" he asked as he shoved the gun into his pocket.

"I already testified. There's nothing else to say."

"Yeah, you do have a big mouth. That's a problem. Got my brother put away. Of course, I'd probably have done the same in your shoes. Luke did off your husband, after all." He leaned against a support beam. "You're a young woman with a kid. You're a good mother, too, protecting your little girl like you are. If it were up to me, I'd be tempted to let you live, but my boss wants to make sure you don't tell anyone what your husband told you. Since he pays the bills, my hands are tied."

She went cold at the words.

Was there more to Joe's murder than she knew? Had he been involved in something else?

"The only thing my husband said was that I needed to keep Sophia safe," she told him, her voice airy and light with fear. "Don't you think I would have already told the police if he'd given me other information?"

"You got a point," the man said, smiling the kind

of smile that said he didn't care. "But it doesn't make any difference. I have my orders, and I'm going to follow them."

"What orders?"

Something thudded overhead.

Saunders's brother swore, his attention shifting for a fraction of a second as he took a step back, looked up at the ceiling.

Annie didn't hesitate, didn't think through anything but sprinting into the darkness, hiding among the equipment. She dived behind a support beam, ran behind heavy-duty machines that must have been there since the turn of the twentieth century.

A shot rang out, the metal near her head vibrating with the force of the impact. Something grazed her cheek, but she kept running, Sophia clinging to her as lights went on all over the room.

Up ahead, a door yawned open, hanging from one hinge.

She ran through it, stumbling into a dark corridor, something sticky and wet sliding down her face. She didn't have time to wipe it away. Doors lined the walls on either side of the hallway. Some open. Some closed. If she went in one, she might be trapped. If she stayed in the hall, she'd be a moving target.

She ducked into a room, shushing Sophia as she scurried deeper into the interior. Moonlight shone through floor-to-ceiling windows, and she could see a door at the far end of the room.

She crept toward it, her heart pounding so loudly that she was sure Saunders's brother would hear it and find her. Long tables filled the room. A break area, maybe, or cafeteria? She didn't know, didn't care. All she wanted to do was find a way to safety.

She could hear footsteps in the corridor, and the hair on the back of her neck stood on end. He was probably checking every room, hunting for her.

If she didn't find a way out, he'd find her.

She ducked through the doorway, found herself in what looked to be a kitchen.

There had to be a way out. A delivery door or something.

She didn't dare turn on a light as she eased through the darkness, making her way past a counter and a sink. There was a window above it. If she could get it open, she could crawl out and run.

"Where we going, Mommy?" Sophia asked, popping her head up.

"Shhhhh," she said, her muscles taut with fear.

Had he entered the room behind her? Was he creeping toward the kitchen?

She felt sick with terror, but she climbed onto the counter, set her feet in the sink. The window was stuck tight, too many layers of paint preventing the lock from opening.

Something rustled in the darkness beyond the

doorway, and her heart nearly burst with fear. If she couldn't get out, she had to be ready to fight.

She jumped off the counter, opened a cupboard beneath the sink. Nothing that she could use as a weapon, but the area was large, and she thought she and Sophia could both fit. Or, maybe, she'd just put Sophia in the cupboard, hide her there until it was safe for her to come out.

"Let's play hide-and-seek, Sophia," she whispered. "Be really, really quiet, okay?"

"Okay," Sophia agreed, but she didn't sound very confident.

If Annie died, would anyone find her daughter? Would Hunter figure out what had happened and come looking?

She kissed Sophia's soft cheek, put her in the cupboard, leaving the door open just a crack so that she wouldn't be scared. She couldn't let anything happen to her daughter. She had to find a weapon, she had to fight and, most important, she had to win.

NINETEEN

Hunter ran down the flight of stairs that led to the basement of the old warehouse, his heart thundering in his ears, the beam from his flashlight bouncing on old marble. Two St. Louis police officers pounded down the steps behind him. They'd planned to enter silently, approach cautiously, but a gunshot had broken the stillness of the building, the sound echoing up from the basement.

Please, Lord, let them be okay, he prayed as he reached the stairwell door. A glass window looked into a long dark corridor. Hunter thought he saw someone moving through the gloom.

He put up his hand, signaling for the officers to approach slowly.

"I think I see our perp," he whispered.

More movement in the hall, and he could make out a few more details. A man, moving cautiously. No sign of anyone else.

Had the bullet found its target?

He refused to let his mind go down that dark path. He had to believe that Annie and Sophia were okay.

He watched as the perp disappeared in a room.

Now was his chance.

He signaled again, opening the door and stepping into the corridor, pressing close to the wall, his body humming with adrenaline. Thank goodness Annie's father and Burke had followed the fleeing suspect. If not, the St. Louis P.D. and U.S. Marshals would still be hunting for Burke's stolen car.

He eased into the room the suspect had disappeared into, heard a loud bang and a sharp curse.

He stepped into the room and flashed his light straight into the eyes of a man who looked so much like Luke Saunders, Hunter could have almost believed they were the same. The guy had one hand pressed to his thigh and the other wrapped around a handgun.

"Drop the weapon," Hunter commanded, his firearm pointed straight at the guy's heart.

The perp released the Glock he'd been holding, letting it fall to the floor with another curse.

"I think I need stitches," he moaned, lifting his hand so that Hunter could see blood bubbling up from a deep cut there. He must have slammed into the edge of one of the metal tables and ripped his leg open.

Hunter had no sympathy for him.

"You're going to need more than that if you don't

put your hands up and leave them where we can see them," one of the officers said.

"I know my rights, and I got a right to medical treatment."

"Trust me," the other police officer responded. "You'll get everything you deserve."

Hunter stepped aside and let them frisk the suspect, read him his Miranda rights and cuff him.

As soon as they finished, he approached. "Where are the Delacortes?"

"I don't know what you're talking about," the perp spat, his dark eyes flashing ire.

"Just like you don't know how one of my men was shot twice or how the gun you were carrying was used to do it?"

"I'm not saying nothing until I have my lawyer," the guy said, pressing his lips together.

It was all Hunter could do not to grab him by the collar and shake the truth out of him.

"We're not playing games here," the older of the two cops barked. "Did you come here alone, or is there someone else working with you?"

The perp smirked and kept his mouth shut.

Hunter clenched his fists to keep from doing something he'd regret. His fault. All of it. He should have stuck with the original plan, refused to go to the prison to meet with Fiske.

That had been a waste of valuable time.

Fiske had insisted that he and Saunders were

working for a guy named Mr. Big. According to him, Mr. Big had hired Saunders's brother to make sure Annie didn't testify.

Saunders's brother *Don.*

No wonder the perp looked familiar.

"Look, Don," he growled and was pleased to see the guy's eyes widen in surprise. "We already know what you're doing and who you're working for. Tell us where the Delacortes are and you might not spend the rest of your life in jail."

"I told you. I got nothing to say," he insisted.

"We'll see how much good that does you once you're booked on attempted-murder charges," Hunter muttered, stalking from the room. He had to find Annie and Sophia. He had to make sure they were okay.

Please, let them be okay.

The younger of the two officers followed him into the hall. "Sergeant Cline is going to take the suspect out to the patrol car. He's calling for a K-9 team. That will make the search easier."

"Agreed, but I don't want to stand around twiddling my thumbs until they get here. Why don't we split up? You head right. I'll go left. Check every room. A shot was fired. We just need to figure out where that happened. And be careful. We don't know if Saunders was working alone. There could be someone else hiding around here."

"Will do." The officer took off.

Hunter made his way down the long hallway, cautiously checking one room after another. Nothing. No sign of a struggle. No hint that Sophia or Annie had been there. He would have called for them, but if there was a second perp hanging around, he didn't want to give advance warning.

A splotch of something gleamed in the beam of his flashlight, and he bent down to examine it.

Blood. He didn't need a forensic team to know it.

He ran the beam of his light along the floor until he found another splotch and another. He followed them into what looked like a cafeteria, where he thought he heard a baby crying.

He cocked his head, the cry so faint he wasn't sure he was really hearing it.

He crept through the room, the sound growing louder as he approached another doorway. He flashed the light in before he crossed the threshold. A kitchen. One window and a long counter. Plenty of cupboards.

A shadow moved to his right, lunging out from beside the large fridge, tackling him with enough force to send him tumbling backward. The flashlight flew from his hand, clattering onto the floor and rolling away.

He fell hard, but managed to twist so he was on top, his hands tight around someone's wrists. Someone's very slender wrists.

Not a man.

A woman.

He could smell her perfume, flowery and light, feel the fabric of her dress scrunching up near his legs.

"Annie," he whispered, releasing her wrists, smoothing his hands up her arms. "Are you okay?"

"Hunter?" Her voice was shaky, and her cheek was bleeding, but she was alive. Thank the Lord.

"A little late but finally here." He pulled her to her feet, his heart pounding with the need to drag her into his arms. "Where's Sophia?"

"I's still hiding," Sophia said, her voice muffled.

"You can come out, sweetie." Annie hurried across the room and opened the cupboard under the sink, lifting Sophia from the darkness.

His muscles went weak with relief, all the icy fear that had been in his heart since Burke called to say that Annie and Sophia had been kidnapped melting away.

He crossed the room in two long strides, pulled them both into his arms. They fit perfectly there, and he knew it was exactly where they were meant to be.

"Thank God," he whispered. "You're both okay."

"Burke isn't. I think he's—"

"Okay. The first bullet grazed his shoulder. The second one creased his scalp. It's a good thing Saunders's brother is a poor shot and that Burke has got such a hard head. He and your dad are the reason why we found you so quickly. They were able to follow Burke's car while Bud called 911. The guy who kidnapped you is already in custody."

"I can't believe it. Burke was out cold when Luke's brother grabbed me. I was sure…" She shook her head. "I'm just glad Burke and my father are okay, and I'm even more glad that you're here." Her arm snaked around his waist, her hand clutching his waistband. "I have never been so scared in my life."

"I'm sorry, Annie. I should never have let you go to dinner without me."

"You couldn't have known this would happen."

"I still—"

"Don't." She pressed a finger to his lips. "I'm okay. Sophia is okay. Tomorrow, we're going off to start our new lives, and we're going to do it knowing that the guy who planted bombs and threatened me is behind bars. That's a wonderful gift, Hunter, and I can't thank you enough for it."

"I don't need you to thank me, Annie," he said, looking into her face, seeing everything he'd ever wanted there.

"Then what do you need?"

"You by my side while *I* start *my* new life."

"Hunter—"

"I'd already decided to take some time off work because I need it and because I can't imagine not having you and Sophia in my life. I'm going to bring you to your new home and help you settle in."

"But—"

He pressed a finger to her lips, sealing in any protest she might have made. "Let's just call it a first step to forever, okay? We don't have to know where it leads—we just have to start the journey."

"I'd...like that," she admitted.

"Then how about we get started?"

She looked into his eyes. He didn't know what she was searching for, but he wanted to give it to her.

"You know what?" she finally said. "I think we should."

He smiled, lifting Sophia from her arms. "How about you, munchkin? You want to find forever with me?"

"And cookies?" she asked.

"That, too," he promised as he linked hands with Annie and led them both from the room.

TWENTY

Obviously, it isn't a straight shot to forever, Annie thought as a doctor stitched the deep gash in her cheek.

She'd thought they'd go to Hunter's house, grab their things and head out. Hunter had insisted they go straight to the hospital.

She was glad. Her parents were both there, playing with Sophia. Seeing them with her was bittersweet. They'd have to say goodbye again, be separated again, but she had to trust that eventually God would bring them back together.

"So, you have to leave us again, huh?" her father, Bill Stanley, said for what seemed like the hundredth time. "You're sure it isn't safe to stick around here?"

"I wish it were, Dad. I've really missed you guys."

"We've missed you, too, but we'd rather have you alive and out of reach than gone forever."

"I know." Annie winced as the doctor jabbed at her cheek.

"I wish we could go with you, honey," her mother

said, a wistfulness in her voice that Annie had never heard before.

"You love it in St. Louis. When I was a kid, you said that you never wanted to leave." She tried to turn her head to see her mother's expression, but the doctor frowned. An on-call plastic surgeon, he'd insisted that he could make sure that Annie's scar was almost unnoticeable.

"Try to hold still. You don't want to have a jagged scar when this heals," he said sternly.

She honestly didn't care. She'd been through a lot of pain and a lot of trial, but she'd survived. A scar on her cheek seemed a fitting reminder of that.

She held still anyway.

"Because you were here," her mother continued. "St. Louis just doesn't seem like home when you're not around."

"You know, Sandy," Bill said. "I can take early retirement. If the marshals would help, maybe we could start over with Annie and Sophia."

"That sounds wonderful," Sandy gushed. "We could be a family again!"

It sounded more than wonderful. It sounded like all the dreams Annie had been afraid to hope for during the past year.

Someone knocked on the door.

"Come in," Annie called.

The door opened, and Hunter walked in. He

looked rugged, handsome and so wonderful that her heart jumped with happiness.

"How are you doing?" he asked, crossing the room in three long strides.

"Better now that you're here."

He smiled and lifted her hand, turning so that he was looking at her family. "I'm sorry this happened to your daughter, Mr. and Mrs. Stanley. I take full responsibility."

"I told you that *I'm* taking responsibility," Burke said as Serena wheeled him into the room. He was pale, his head bandaged, his T-shirt pulled tight over his bandaged shoulder. "If I'd parked in the driveway, this wouldn't have happened. I'm a failure as a marshal. I need to resign."

"It's getting awfully crowded in here," the doctor sighed as he applied a bandage to the wound. "You're all set. I'll have the nurse come in with aftercare instructions." He glanced around the room, sighed again and walked out.

"Like I was saying," Burke continued, his words slurring slightly. "I'm going to hand in my resignation as soon as I get back to the office."

"You're still loopy from the drugs they gave you, Burke. So shut up and stop having your pity party," Serena said, but she pulled a blanket up a little higher on his lap and patted his uninjured shoulder.

"I'm not—"

"You can't resign. I'm taking extended leave beginning tomorrow," Hunter cut in. "I'm not sure when or if I'll be back."

"Why not just take a vacation?" Josh walked into the room, skirting by Serena and the wheelchair. "You haven't had one in years."

"Because I really don't think I'm coming back." Hunter squeezed Annie's hand, looked down into her eyes. She didn't want him to give up his job for her, but she wanted him happy, and right then, she could see all the joy on his face.

He felt good about his decision. Right about it.

She couldn't feel any other way.

The group of marshals looked stunned.

"Did you hire that Colton Philips guy?" Burke asked, a scowl etching deep lines on his face. "Because it sounds like we're going to need him."

"I spoke to him a couple of times, but I think he's too brash for our team. The three of you will do fine until a replacement can be found. Bud Hollingsworth said he'll do whatever he can during the transition."

Serena sighed. "Daniel's gone. You're leaving. The office is going to be empty."

"Not empty. Josh will be there, and so will I. I obviously can't resign until we get someone to take Hunter's place," Burke griped, but he looked relieved rather than upset.

"It's not like I'll be out of contact," Hunter assured the team. "I'll be as close as a phone call if you need to consult with me. We still have to find out who was leaking information to Don Saunders."

"Or to his boss," Annie said without thinking.

The room went completely silent. Even Sophia stopped babbling and squealing.

"What do you mean?" Hunter asked quietly.

"He made a phone call to someone he called 'boss.' He told him that I wouldn't tell anyone anything ever again." She explained the rest quickly.

When she was done, Josh let out a long low whistle. "It sounds like your husband knew something that he didn't share with you. We're going to have to do some more digging to find out what."

"Maybe visiting Fiske wasn't a waste of time after all," Hunter added. "He mentioned a boss, too. Some guy he called Mr. Big. I thought he made it up, but maybe the guy really exists. The officers who booked Saunders called me a few minutes ago. They said he hasn't stopped talking. He insists he has information that we need."

"What kind of information?" Josh asked.

"Something about a baby-smuggling ring." His gaze shot to Sophia.

"Are you saying that the men who murdered Joe were trying to snatch my daughter?" Had Joe been protecting Sophia? Was that why he'd died?

"We don't have all the information yet, but we're keeping the arrest quiet. We don't want any information leaked out. If he's right, the less information Mr. Big has, the better it will be for the investigation."

"But—" She wanted to ask a million more questions, try to wrap her mind around the new information, but Josh cut her off.

"I think I'll pay Fiske a visit tomorrow, see if I can get any more information out of him," he said.

"Keep me posted, okay?" Hunter responded. "I may be taking a leave of absence, but I want to know what's going on."

"That being the case, you've been careful with information regarding where she's relocating to, right?" Serena said, shooting a look at Annie's parents.

"Very," Hunter responded.

"Glad to hear it. We've gotten them this far. I don't want anything to happen to them now that the trial is over. Come on, Burke. I'm supposed to get you home and make sure you don't kill yourself climbing into bed."

"I'd better head out, too. I want to go over the Delacorte files, see if there's anything in there we missed." Josh followed Serena out of the room.

"I thought this was over," Bill said, taking Annie's hand and squeezing gently. "I thought you were finally going to be safe."

"She will be," Hunter assured him. "I'm going to make sure of it."

"What can we do to help?" Sandy carried Sophia over.

"Pray and wait for an opportunity to join your daughter and granddaughter." He took Sophia from her arms, and Annie's heart swelled with love as she looked at the two of them together. They looked comfortable together, happy together.

They looked like a family together.

"So, you think that might be a possibility? Because I really don't want to go the rest of my life without seeing my daughter and granddaughter again." Sandy's eyes welled with tears.

"I already have it in the works. As soon as you're ready—"

"We're ready," Annie's father cut in.

"The marshals will arrange everything, then. You should be able to join us in a few weeks."

"*Us?* So, there's going to be a wedding?" Bill asked, his brow furrowed into a million lines.

"Dad!" Annie cut in quickly. "I'm going to have my own place. Hunter will be...?" What would he be doing?

She met his eyes, and he smiled. "I'll find a place to rent for a while."

"Oh. Okay, then." Bill nodded. "Glad to hear it. Now it seems to me, the best thing for my daughter and granddaughter would be to get them out of town quickly."

"That's what I intend to do."

"Then we'll say goodbye. Hopefully, it won't be for long," Bill said, kissing Annie's uninjured cheek and pulling her in for a bear hug. She swallowed back tears, pasting a smile on her face as she said goodbye. Again.

"You okay?" Hunter asked after her parents walked out of the room.

"I think so." She ran a hand over her hair, pulling out pins that were barely holding it into place. "It's just really hard to say goodbye again."

"It'll only be for a few months." He put Sophia down, ruffling her hair as he gazed straight into Annie's eyes.

"I know."

"Then why do you look so sad?"

"Because I've missed them, and they've already missed so much of Sophia's life."

"I'm sorry," he murmured, slipping his arms around her waist, his lips grazing her forehead, so lightly, so tenderly, tears filled her eyes.

"It's not your fault. It's all because of Joe. Everything that happened is because he—"

"May have saved her, Annie. If what Saunders told the police is true, he probably did," Hunter said gently, his hand cupping her jaw, his eyes warm and brown and filled with promises. "Let's make sure we tell her that when she's older. I want her to have good feelings about her first father."

"First?"

"Sure. I kind of liked your father's suggestion about having a wedding. I was hoping that, in a few months, there might just be one."

"You know what?" she said, placing her hand over the one he'd rested against her waist. "I think I like that idea."

"Think?" he asked with a small laugh. "I'd rather you be sure."

"I am," she whispered, leaning forward and sealing the words with a kiss that she felt to the depth of her soul. "You're everything I was afraid to hope for after Joe died."

"And you're everything I didn't know I needed but do. I love you, Annie."

"I love you, too," she murmured against his lips.

"I loves you, Hunter! I loves you!" Sophia cried.

Hunter broke away, laughing as he scooped Sophia into his arms.

"I'm glad to hear it, munchkin, because I plan to stick around for a long time. Come on." He slipped his free arm around Annie's waist. "Let's go back to my place and pack. I'm ready for our forever to begin."

"So am I, Hunter," Annie said, her heart nearly bursting with joy as they stepped out into the hall and walked into their future together.

* * * * *

Dear Reader,

I was so excited when I was asked to be part of the 2014 Harlequin Love Inspired Suspense continuity! I love working with other authors. I also enjoy taking someone else's story idea and making it my own. As I delved into the world of U.S. Marshals and witness protection, I often found myself wondering what it would be like to be on the run, cut off from everyone and everything I know and love.

Annie Duncan—aka Angel Delacorte—has given up her family, her friends and her job to testify against the men who murdered her husband. She's in hiding with her young daughter, and she feels more alone than she's ever been. U.S. marshal Hunter Davis has always played by the rules, keeping his emotions separated from his job. When he's assigned to Annie's case, he doesn't expect things to be any different. But there's something about Annie that he can't resist. As the two face down a hidden enemy, they must rely on their faith and each other to see them through.

Blessings,

Shirlee McCoy

Questions for Discussion

1. Annie gave up her family, friends and everything she's ever known in order to testify against her husband's killer. Why did she make that choice?

2. Is there any point at which Annie regrets her decision?

3. Joe embodied all of Annie's hopes and dreams. What did she think she would attain by marrying him?

4. What did she lose by marrying Joe? What do you think she gained?

5. Have you ever known someone with an addiction? How did it impact your relationship?

6. What are Annie's first impressions of Hunter?

7. When does she begin to see him in a different light?

8. Why is Hunter so determined to stay single? Describe the relationship his parents had and how that has impacted his life.

9. Hunter makes his job his first priority. How does that change as the story progresses?

10. How would you describe Annie's marriage and her husband? How do you think that relationship changed her?

11. What is it about Hunter that appeals to Annie?

12. At one point in the book, Annie jumps out of a moving car to get to her daughter. Would you have done the same? Explain.

13. There's a leak within the U.S. Marshals that has yet to be revealed. Who do you think it is? Why?

14. At the end of the book, it becomes clear that there was more going on the night of Joe's murder than anyone originally thought. Do you think Joe was killed because he was protecting Sophia from kidnappers? If so, how might that change Annie's perspective?

15. Who was your favorite character and why?

LARGER-PRINT BOOKS!

GET 2 FREE
LARGER-PRINT NOVELS
PLUS 2 FREE
MYSTERY GIFTS

Love Inspired®
SUSPENSE
RIVETING INSPIRATIONAL ROMANCE

Larger-print novels are now available...

LISLPDIR13R

LARGER-PRINT BOOKS!

GET 2 FREE
LARGER-PRINT NOVELS
PLUS 2 FREE
MYSTERY GIFTS

Love Inspired

Larger-print novels are now available...